Féile Fever

JOE O'BRIEN is an award-winning gardener who lives in Ballyfermot, Dublin. He is the author of the first book about GAA player, Danny Wilde, *Little Croker*. He is also the author of the popular *Alfie Green* series for younger readers.

Féile Fever

Joe O'Brien

THE O'BRIEN PRESS
DUBLIN

First published 2009 by The O'Brien Press Ltd,
12 Terenure Road East, Rathgar, Dublin 6, Ireland.
Tel: +353 1 4923333; Fax: +353 1 4922777
E-mail: books@obrien.ie
Website: www.obrien.ie

ISBN: 978-1-84717-173-3

British Library Cataloguing in Publication Data
A catalogue record for this title is available from the British Library

1 2 3 4 5 6 7 8
09 10 11 12 13

The O'Brien Press receives
assistance from

Layout and design: The O'Brien Press Ltd
Printed and bound in the UK by CPI Group Ltd.
Cover photo © copyright Sportsfile.

Mixed Sources
Product group from well-managed
forests and other controlled sources
www.fsc.org Cert no. TT-COC-002227
© 1996 Forest Stewardship Council

Dedication

For my cousin, and dear friend, Michael.

Author's Note

When I decided to write another book about Danny Wilde
and his team's promotion to the Under-14s Division, I didn't
initially think of including the Féile. However, after research-
ing the Féile and discovering its importance to GAA, both in
Ireland and in other GAA-hooked countries, I'm thrilled that I
did!

I feel that the Féile is a symbol of the great GAA spirit that
stretches from the highest levels right down to local
communities, enhancing the lives of all the participants.
I hope you enjoy reading about Danny's Féile experience
in this book.

Joe O'Brien

Acknowledgements

As always, I'd like to thank everyone at The O'Brien Press for their support and hard work, especially my editor, Helen Carr, Emma Byrne for the wonderful book design, Ruth Heneghan for all her hard work promoting my books, Ivan O'Brien, Brenda Boyne and all the sales team for their support and hard work. Special thanks must go to Mary Webb, Editorial Director, for encouraging me to write these sports books and Michael O'Brien, Publisher, for being the great person he is and for giving me the opportunity to be an author.

Big thanks once again to Paul Faughnan of St Patrick's GAA Club, Palmerstown, for all his valuable GAA advice and information, and for giving me so much of his time.

I would also like to thank Kevin Nicol for his fascinating tour of Croke Park (which I would highly recommend) and John Costello (County Board Secretary) for his kind welcome and words of wisdom at Parnell Park.

Sincere thanks to all the supportive booksellers and librarians, and all who dedicate so much of their time to the world of books.

A huge thanks to the staff at Ballyfermot Library for looking after me so well and finding me cosy, quiet corners while I was writing this book.

Once again, thanks to TG4 for their comprehensive coverage of GAA games, which I enjoyed while writing both *Féile Fever* and *Little Croker*.

Last, but certainly not least, sincere thanks to my wife, Mandy, and my son, Jamie – I love and adore them more than anything in the world (even writing, and that's saying a lot!).

Contents

Chapter One

The Match Against Chapel Hall

'When you go out onto that pitch, lads, where are you playing?' cried Mick.

'The Little Croker!' replied the team.

'And how do you play every game?' asked Mick.

'LIKE THE ALL-IRELAND FINAL!' cheered the whole dressing room.

Then with a familiar clatter of studs, the team raced out onto the pitch like an army going into battle.

It was Saturday 25 April and Littlestown Crokes were playing at home against league-leaders Chapel Hall. Even though the Crokes were finding their promotion to Under-14's

Division 1 difficult, only picking up five points out of a possible ten in their first five games, Danny Wilde led his team out onto the Little Croker with his head held high.

Crokes had beaten Barnfield in last season's Under-13's Division 2 league, and Danny's winner's medal was sitting polished and proud on the mantelpiece back home, but neither Danny nor Mick could work out exactly why Barnfield were settling into Division 1 so much better. This bothered the father and son – the Crokes' coach and captain – big time.

Today was a huge test for Mick's team. Chapel Hall, last year's Under-13's Division 1 winners, were already looking like runaway league leaders, and they proved that in the first twenty minutes of the match, hammering over six points and playing as if *they*, and not the Crokes, were all-Ireland finalists.

Danny and his cousin Jonathon battled their hearts out in midfield, but every time they managed to get the ball up to their forward line, the

Chapel Hall defence was too strong. By the half-time whistle, Chapel Hall had scored a goal and two more points. Even though Danny had knocked over a wonderful long point after going on one of his special Danny solos, and Barry Sweeney, Crokes' centre full forward, had added two points to Danny's, Mick was faced with fifteen deflated Littlestown warriors at half-time, trailing by a score of 0-3 to 1-8.

'Gather them in, Jimmy,' instructed Mick.

'Come on, boys!' said Jimmy, Mick's assistant, clapping his hands a few times to get the players' attention.

Larry, Mick's brother and Jonathon's dad, was strolling back down the line. He had Danny's dog, Heffo, the team mascot, with him; Heffo was twirling around in circles trying his best to eat his lead. Alan Whelan, Crokes' centre half back and big Johnner Purcell, the full back were laughing at Heffo and paying absolutely no attention to Jimmy.

Suddenly everyone around the pitch jumped

to attention as Mick Wilde blew hard on his whistle.

'Right, lads, are yiz *listening* or will we all just go home now?'

Everyone, including Jimmy and Larry, gathered in a circle around Mick. Even Heffo didn't dare take his eyes off his master as Mick delivered his half-time words of wisdom.

'I know yiz are struggling in this division, lads, but you have it in you to compete with these guys,' encouraged Mick. 'You just have to knuckle in and believe in yourselves. Barry,' said Mick as he glanced over at his centre full forward, 'great points, son. You've scored in every game so far this season. Get me more of them. And well done, Danny, and you too, Jonathon. Don't be afraid to take them on and run at them. I know their defence is strong, but don't be afraid to shoulder them off.'

'That's right boys. Get stuck into them. Show them what you're made of,' added Larry.

Jimmy rolled his eyes at Larry and then

rolled them up to the heavens, making sure that Mick saw him doing it.

Who does he think he is, interrupting Mick like that, thought Jimmy, *I never interrupted Mick during his half-time talk and I'm assistant coach. Flamin' cheek. Things were better when him and Mick hated each other. He wasn't around to interfere then.*

Mick managed a discreet supportive smile at Jimmy, who he knew had become a little jealous of Larry's new-found interest in his son's team.

Suddenly the ref's whistle blew, it was time for the teams to get back onto the pitch.

Mick made one substitution and brought on Derek Moran to replace Paul Kiely, who was having a terrible game at right half forward.

'Come on the Crokes!' shouted Jimmy, as the boys took up their positions on the field.

'Come on there, boys!' cheered Larry. 'Get in there from the start!'

Jimmy looked at Mick again.

'I think I'll bring Heffo for a walk now,' he said.

'Will you relax!' whispered Mick, smiling. 'They need all the support they can get.'

Deep down, Mick knew that Crokes needed more than just support if they were to get anything out of this game.

The referee threw the ball high in the air and Danny Wilde jumped for that ball as if he was jumping on behalf of every single one of his players. Taking his dad's advice on board from the very start of the second-half, Danny shouldered his opponent off him as his feet landed back on the crisp turf and he swiftly fisted the ball to Jonathon.

Jonathon then fisted a high pass over the other Chapel Hall centre midfielder sending the ball back into the hands of his captain. Once again, Danny Wilde went on a Danny solo, twisting and shimmying around the Chapel Hall players as if he was a ghost player, untouchable and unstoppable.

Doyler, Crokes' centre half forward pulled his player out wide and opened up a gap for Danny as he approached the heart of Chapel Hall's defence.

Barry Sweeney was battling with his marker to try and shake him off, but the full back was stuck to Barry like super glue. Then, with an extra burst of effort, Barry shrugged off the number 3 and headed for goal, just as Danny lobbed a perfect pass towards him. Barry fisted the ball into the back of the net, clashed with Chapel Hall's goalkeeper and went crashing to the ground in a tangle of arms and legs.

'GOAL!!' cheered Jimmy, and he danced up and down the line.

The Crokes supporters went wild!

'Barry's not getting up!' announced Larry suddenly to Mick.

'Water, Jimmy,' instructed Mick as he ran across the pitch to the stricken player.

The celebrations came to an abrupt end as the spectators became aware that Barry was lying in agony on the ground, holding his collarbone and crying in pain.

No amount of water was going to fix this injury, and Mick knew straight away that there was a real chance that his in-form number fourteen had sustained a broken collar bone from the clash with the goal keeper.

Danny ushered his team away from the scene and instructed them back to their positions.

Mick and Jimmy managed to get Barry to his feet and helped him over to the sidelines. The referee and Chapel Hall's manager followed them over.

'I think he needs to go to hospital,' said the referee.

'I'll ring an ambulance,' said Jimmy.

'I'm not getting into the back of an ambulance,' screeched Barry.

'You have to, son,' said the other team's manager.

'No way!' insisted Barry.

'I'll take him in my car,' offered Larry, seeing

that Barry was getting more and more upset at the suggestion of an ambulance being called.

'I'll go too,' said Mick.

Jimmy looked relieved. The thought of having to sit beside Larry in the car was too much to bear, but then suddenly the thought of having to finish out this awful game without Mick seemed worse.

'Are you sure, Mick? I can go,' said Jimmy. 'Sure you stay here for the rest of the match.'

Mick Wilde wasn't having any of it. He was the manager and one of his players was hurt. It was his place to be with Barry.

*   *   *

A good fifteen minutes had passed and the buzz of Crokes scoring their goal had fizzled out completely.

Jimmy brought on little John Watson to play in centre half forward and Doyler pushed up into Barry's position – centre full forward.

Even though Crokes tried their best to stay in touch with their opponents, Barry's exit had weakened their attacking power.

Jonathon managed to score a point, as did Jimmy's son, Splinter, bringing Crokes' score up to one goal and five points, but Chapel Hall surpassed their efforts by adding a further three points to their score.

To make matters worse, just as Danny had knocked the ball out wide to Splinter, with an amazing hook kick from the outside of his right foot, and Splinter had turned his marker to shoot for a point, an unusual disturbance to the far side of the pitch caused Splinter to miskick his shot, sending it far wide of the posts.

Billy Stapleton, a boy from Danny and Splinter's class in school, charged onto the Little Croker on the back of a horse, with two park rangers chasing him.

'Get out of the way!' roared Billy, as he skillfully guided the horse around all the players.

Danny was *furious* and poor Jimmy was

mortified. Jimmy and Mick always prided themselves on the good reputation that Littlestown had when it came to GAA. It was one of the good things going for the area, and now here was young Billy tearing across Mick's arena, making a mockery of it and letting down Littlestown in front of the opposing team.

'What's the story, Danny?' shouted Billy, 'all right, Splinter?'

'Get off the pitch, ye muppet!' yelled Danny. He could hear all the Chapel Hall supporters laughing from the sideline.

The referee had had enough. He put his whistle to his mouth and blew on it as hard as he could.

The match finished 1-5 to 1-11 in Chapel Hall's favour.

As Billy Stapleton rode off into the distance and the clouds began to pour rivers of rain down, all the Crokes and Chapel Hall players ran to the dressing rooms.

Danny and Splinter helped Jimmy take down

the nets, then slowly made their way off the pitch, leaving it all alone; worn and battered and empty and humiliated.

It was a dismal day on the Little Croker.

Chapter Two

New Boy

On Tuesday morning in maths class, Danny and Splinter were tearing ribbons out of Billy Stapleton, who sat in front of them.

Mr Breen had popped out for a few minutes, leaving the class to revise for a maths test the next day.

Splinter rolled up one of his copybooks and smacked Billy on the back of the head. Billy jumped and turned around, rubbing his hair.

'What was that for, ye nutter?'

'You're calling *me* a nutter when you were the headcase ripping across the pitch on Saturday with your flea-infested donkey!' laughed Splinter.

'Shut up, you,' tutted Billy, 'That horse is a pure bred.'

Billy loved his horse and spent nearly all his time over at the Littlestown Community Stables with him.

Danny was very quiet during the two boys' banter. He was very annoyed with Billy, and was picking his moment to let loose at him.

'Are you finished, ye plank?' growled Danny.

Splinter leaned back in his chair. He knew what was coming, and he didn't want Danny to think that he was taking it all too light-heartedly.

'Who are you calling a plank? Some people know me as Billy the Kid. Did you see them big eejits chasing me yesterday? I ran them around the whole of the park and they still couldn't catch me. Billy the Kid, that's me. Untouch-able!'

'You and your horse won't be untouchable when my da catches up with you.'

Billy's face paled.

'That's right,' Splinter backed Danny up, 'my da told Mick everything about how you made a show of us, and he went crazy!'

Suddenly Billy didn't feel too well. He didn't want Mick Wilde coming over to his house and telling his parents what he'd been up to. He quickly changed the subject.

'I hear poor oul' Barry Sweeney broke his collarbone in three places. That was bad luck, lads. That'll damage your title hopes.'

Before Danny had a chance to reply, Mr Breen came back into the room, and he wasn't alone. Walking behind the maths teacher was the school principal, Mr Dunstan.

'Now boys! Pay attention,' said Mr Breen, hushing the random chat that spread from row to row. 'Principal Dunstan has an announcement to make.'

Mr Dunstan was known throughout the school as 'The Grim Reaper'.

He was tall and thin, and his face was deathly

pale, with dark, hollow eyes. He always wore dark suits and walked in a slow, stiff, military style, as if he was pacing behind a hearse. Because he looked so stern and serious, new pupils always expected Mr Dunstan to have a loud, ear-piercing bellow of a voice, but instead he almost whispered his words – in a screeching whisper that sounded like he'd just eaten a pupil for breakfast!

'*Dia dhuit,*' whispered Principal Dunstan.

Before the class had time to reply, a boy popped out from behind the headmaster.

'Jeepers! Where did he come from?' giggled Splinter.

A few kids sitting near Danny and Splinter laughed, but most of the boys tried to keep straight faces in front of the principal.

Principal Dunstan glared down at Splinter. He didn't need to say a word; his glare was enough to make Splinter fall silent and sink down in his seat.

'Now, boys,' he said then, 'I want you all to

put your hands together and give a kind and hearty Irish welcome to a new pupil who is starting in your class.'

Everybody just stared. Nobody made a single attempt to put their hands together.

'Come on now, boys, Todd here has come all the way from Down Under. Surely we can show him we're a nice bunch of guys?' said Mr Breen.

That kind of worked. Some kids clapped and then some more joined in.

The new boy, Todd, began to turn red under his tan.

The Grim Reaper went on to tell the whole class that Todd had come all the way from Australia and that every pupil in the class should do their very best to make him feel at home.

Danny could see Todd make a rebellious gesture in Mr Dunstan's direction as if to say, *Get real, enough with the intro. I'm bored already. Don't totally make me unpopular.*

Mr Breen guided Todd down to his seat,

which happened to be right in front of Danny and Splinter, beside Billy 'The Kid' Stapleton

As Principal Dunstan and Mr Breen stepped outside for some discussion, Danny, Splinter and Billy didn't hesitate to interrogate Todd.

'So, you're from Down Under?' giggled Billy.

Todd didn't respond. In fact, he didn't even lift his head to look at Billy.

Danny could see that Todd wasn't going to settle in easily, so he pushed Billy's arm,

'Snap out of it, Billy' said Danny. 'Will you give him a chance to settle before you smother him with your sad-act humour.'

The new boy gave a slight smile. Billy noticed this and decided to try a bit more chat.

'So! Come here, Todd,' he said, 'what's the story? Dunstan said that you're from Down Under. Does he mean you're from the Pit of Hell?'

Todd just answered 'right' in his Australian accent and then bowed his head again.

Billy was lucky that Mr Breen walked back

into the classroom and closed the door behind him, as Danny was just about to flick Billy's ear with his ruler to show him that he was being a complete idiot towards Todd.

*　　*　　*

Danny and Splinter were out in the yard having a quick kick-about when they spotted Todd sitting under the shelters, all alone.

'Come on and we'll go over to Todd,' suggested Danny.

'I don't know, Danny,' huffed Splinter. 'He's a bit weird.'

Danny laughed at Splinter.

'He's not *weird*, he's just new. Come on, let's see if we can get to know a bit more about him.'

Splinter slowly followed Danny over to the shelters. Danny sat on one side of Todd and Splinter sat on the other. It was like good cop, bad cop.

'Alright, Todd?' smiled Danny.

Todd didn't answer. He just nodded.

'Come *on*, Danny,' urged Splinter. 'There's only a few minutes of break left.'

Danny didn't want to give up on this new boy. *But maybe he needs time and space, and then he'll come running after us to make friends*, he thought.

Just as the two boys were about to get up, they saw the principal coming across the schoolyard in their direction.

'Ah, no! What's *he* want?' moaned Splinter.

To Danny's delight and Splinter's disgust, Todd laughed.

'Well! If it isn't the Three Amigos,' said Principal Dunstan, with a pitiful attempt at a smile. 'I see you've already made new friends, Todd.'

Todd turned and looked at Danny and Splinter, then nodded at the principal.

'Well, boys. I have some great news for you.'

Then Mr Dunstan paused and looked off around the yard. This was no surprise to

Danny and Splinter as they were well used to his peculiar ways, but Todd just stared at him as if he was looking at a complete alien as he waited to hear what the good news was.

'Your class,' continued the principal, 'has won the surprise school field trip. You'll be going on a day out before the end of term!'

'Savage! I mean, that's super!' cheered Splinter.

Danny smiled at Splinter's enthusiasm; he knew well that Splinter was only so enthusiastic because it meant a day out of the classroom.

'Where's the trip to?' asked Danny.

There was no immediate reply to Danny's question.

Mr Dunstan leaned over towards the three boys with the same expression on his face that he wore at all times.

Danny and Splinter waited patiently. Todd stared at him again, surprised at the way he was able to lean forward with both of his hands in his pockets, balancing on the tips of his toes.

Then out of the blue, he spoke again.

'Croke Park,' whispered the principal.

Danny jumped off the bench.

'Croker!! Why are we going there?'

'You're going on the tour of Croke Park, boys. There's great history in that stadium. A tour well worth taking.'

Danny and Splinter high fived with pure delight.

Just as the, now slightly more popular, school principal was about to turn and walk away, Todd spoke,

'Bonzer! Is this trip on the tin roof?'

Danny and Splinter laughed at Todd.

'Ye mad thing, ye!' said Splinter. 'What language was *that* in?'

'Just kidding with him,' answered Todd, 'I asked him if the trip was free.'

Then he stood up and headed back towards the school, smiling just a little, just enough to tell the two boys that maybe he could fit in after all.

Chapter Three

An Aussie Rules Player

Later that day, Danny, Splinter and Jonathon were having a game of Kick and Catch on Danny's road, to kill some time before training.

Every Tuesday and Thursday, Jonathon got the bus from his school to Danny's house before training. Mick was delighted for Danny to have the company; it had been just the two of them since Danny's mother had died when he was very young, and he sometimes worried that Danny was lonely in the afternoons when he was at work.

Jonathon sat on Danny's wall as he watched his cousin trash Splinter.

'Ah! I think I'll pack it in, Danny,' groaned

Splinter eventually. 'I'll be here all night, trying to beat you.'

'I'll give you a game, Danny,' said Jonathon, and he leapt off the wall.

Just as Danny and Jonathon prepared to play, Deco Savage and Sean Dempsey turned the corner. Both boys played for the Crokes' rivals, Barnfield, and neither of them was at all popular with Danny or his team-mates. Sean Dempsey, in particular, was no friend of Danny's, as Mick had kicked him off the Crokes' team last year for dirty tactics.

'Here! Giz a game?' Dempsey called out.

Jonathon looked at Danny with an *Are you on for it?* look.

'Animal!' replied Danny. 'Kick and catch. Me against Deco, and J against you. One player will kick and the other two have to catch, then we switch it around.'

Danny stayed where he was, while Jonathon and Dempsey ran about three houses down the road, to get ready to catch the ball.

Danny kicked first and sent the ball high above the catchers. Jonathan leapt high and managed to grab the ball out of the sky. Dempsey was slightly taller than Jonathon, but although Jonathon wasn't as good at winning balls in the air as Danny, he was better than Dempsey!

First point to Danny and Jonathon.

Dempsey kicked next, and Danny and Savage contested.

Danny caught that one – two nil to Danny and Jonathon!

Sean 'Dirty' Dempsey got it into his head that there was no way he was going to be humiliated in the middle of the road, so he decided to up his game, and the only way he knew how to do that was to play dirty.

It was Deco Savage's turn to kick and he kicked it very high indeed.

Jonathon timed his jump to perfection.

Dempsey waited and waited and just as it seemed that he'd fallen asleep – THUMP! – he knocked Jonathon out of the way in mid flight and caught the ball.

'Ouch!' yelped Jonathon, as he fell awkwardly on his ankle.

Danny ran over to him.

'Are you alright, J?'

'I'm fine!' panted his cousin. He was obviously in some pain, but tried to keep a brave face in front of Dempsey and Savage.

'Cop on, Dempsey, will ya!' raged Danny.

'Get stuffed!' retaliated Dempsey, as he tried to play the innocent, but Danny wasn't having any of it.

'There's no need for dirt.'

'That wasn't dirt!' interrupted Deco, 'That was a fair tackle, man. Are we playing on or what?'

'I don't think I *can* play on, Danny,' admitted Jonathon. 'I can feel my ankle swelling up.'

'Ah, come *on*, you windbag!' slagged Dempsey. 'It wasn't that bad.'

Splinter jumped off the wall where he had

been watching the whole incident very carefully.

'I'll play instead, and then we'll see who's a windbag.'

But just as Splinter spoke, another contestant for this very heated game turned up.

'I'll jump in if that's alright?'

It was Todd Bailey, the new Aussie boy! He'd been watching the whole game from the corner of Danny and Splinter's road.

Danny nodded at Splinter. Splinter knew what was on Danny's mind, and he too was mad keen to see the mysterious Todd in action.

'Go ahead, Todd,' he said.

'Next point the winner!' announced Danny.

Danny knew Sean Dempsey well, as he'd played alongside him for long enough and he knew in his heart that Dempsey would do whatever it took to win this game.

On the other hand, he was faced with the problem of not knowing Todd at all, but he would just have to trust Todd to bring the points home and send Sean Dempsey and Deco Savage back to Barnfield with their tails between their legs.

Deco won the toss of a coin to throw in.

The Barnfield midfielder looked at his team mate and seemed to make a signal.

Dempsey picked up the signal and grinned.

Savage kicked the ball short and not too high.

Dempsey stepped forward to catch it, but just as the ball was coming down right on target, Todd Bailey swooped up behind Dempsey and leapt in the air, landing almost on his opponent's shoulders, to catch the ball.

Dempsey tumbled to the hard ground with Todd behind him, but somehow Todd kept the ball glued to his hands.

Danny, Splinter and Jonathon leapt about in celebration, then Jonathon quickly sat back down on the kerb again, remembering his injured ankle.

'That was a foul!' shouted Dempsey as he brushed himself off, getting back up.

Todd stood very tall and very strong with the ball in his hands.

'No it wasn't, mate!' he smiled. 'Don't be a possum. That was a mark.'

Just as Dempsey was about to take the disagreement further, Mick drove up the road. As Dempsey was not a favourite of Mick's, he decided very promptly that he and his friend should head off before Mick got out of his car.

Todd fisted the ball over to Danny.

'Here you go, mate. I'm gonna take off now. Thanks for the game.' Then he turned to leave.

'Hold your horses, Todd,' called Danny. 'Aussie rules! That's what that move was. You're good. You could play GAA for our team.'

Todd didn't hang around to take up Danny's offer, and he disappeared back around the corner leaving the three boys feeling nothing but pure admiration for his display of talent.

As Mick got out of his car, he called Danny over.

'Back in a minute, lads,' said Danny, leaving Splinter and Jonathon sitting on the wall.

'Was that Sean Dempsey running off?' asked Mick.

Danny nodded.

'What did he want? Was he giving you grief?'

'No he wasn't, Da. We were playing football and Dempsey and Savage asked for a game. We slaughtered them,' grinned Danny.

'Keep away from those two,' ordered Mick. 'They're bad news. I don't want you hanging around with them.'

'I don't,' said Danny. 'It was a one off. The only time I see Dempsey is at training for the Dublin development squad.'

Mick looked up to the sky in exasperation.

'Is he still in the squad? I can't believe they let Jonathon go and kept Sean Dempsey.'

'I know,' agreed Danny. 'Jonathon was doing really well. I thought he played much better than Dempsey in the Easter tournament.'

Mick walked toward the house, then

turned back to Danny.

'Who was the other lad?'

'What other lad?'

'The big lad that you were talking to a few minutes ago, as I was driving up the road.'

Danny's face lit up.

'That's Todd!' answered Danny with great enthusiasm. 'He's a new lad in our class. He's from Australia.'

'Australia. Really!' smiled Mick. 'He looked older than you, son. They sure know how to grow them down there. All that good sun.'

'You should have seen him, Da. He joined in the game and he *skinned* Dempsey.'

Mick raised a brow.

'He's a player?'

'He's savage,' smiled Danny. 'He pulled off this Aussie Rules move. A mark, that's the one. Dempsey didn't know what hit him!'

In an instant, Mick Wilde's managerial brain switched on.

'Can you ask him to come training?'

'I'll try, Da, but he's not really that easy to get on with.'

'Give him a chance, son. He's only new to Ireland. Probably missing his pals back home.'

'I'll ask him tomorrow in school,' suggested Danny.

'Nice one,' smiled Mick. 'We could really do with putting a bit of strength back into the team after losing poor Barry.'

Mick turned the key in the door.

'Don't stay out too long. I'm going to put on a bit of dinner for you and Jonathon before training.'

Chapter Four

The Barbeque

All that week at school Danny hounded Todd to come training for the Crokes, but Todd wasn't having any of it.

Danny couldn't work out this new lad at all. Todd wasn't exactly the easiest person to make friends with, but Danny Wilde wasn't going to give up on him, and so, even though he couldn't persuade Todd to join his football team, he at least managed to get him to agree to come to a barbeque at his cousin Jonathon's house.

Splinter was going too, and he had cracked a joke to Todd about how the Aussies were the Kings of Barbeques and said that Todd just couldn't refuse to go. So after some resistance,

Todd agreed to tag along, if only to get Splinter and Danny off his case.

*   *   *

Just as Danny had been totally gob-smacked by Jonathon's house the very first time he set eyes on it, Todd Bailey strolled around the immense gardens of number ten Aylesbridge Close with his eyes wide with amazement.

He had been to many barbeques back home, but never in such grand surroundings.

It was Saturday, May 2nd and the bank holiday sun was splitting the stones.

Larry was in tremendous form. When he wasn't working hard as a barrister or playing golf, he loved nothing more than to entertain and show off his lovely home and gardens.

It didn't take very long for Danny to suggest that he and Jonathon show Splinter and Todd the tennis courts hidden in the far garden through the rose arch.

Jonathon's older sister, Lowry, was playing a game with her best friend, Trinity – the girl who Danny had a bit of a soft spot for.

'Who's the bird with the long blonde hair?' asked Splinter.

'That's Trinity,' answered Jonathon. 'The other one is my sister, Lowry.'

'She's eye candy, lads,' laughed Splinter. 'What do you think Todd?'

Todd raised his brows in agreement. 'I reckon she's a beauty, alright!'

Danny wasn't impressed.

'Shut up will yiz, and let's watch the game!'

The four pals sat down and watched the two girls playing for a while.

'They're not bad,' observed Splinter, just as Trinity hit a winning pass; Splinter put his fingers to his mouth and whistled at her.

Trinity and Lowry looked over toward the steps where the boys were sitting. They hadn't noticed them there up until Splinter's outburst.

Lowry made a sort of *get moving or else* gesture

at Jonathon, but Trinity just smiled.

She liked the idea of sideline admirers, and Todd had really caught her eye. He was different. Bronzed, blond haired and blue-eyed.

'I think she was smiling at you, Todd,' said Splinter.

Jonathon noticed Danny's head dropping a little.

'No! You're wrong Splinter,' argued Jonathon. 'I think it was Danny she was smiling at. Trinity likes Danny.'

Danny's face went as red as a tomato.

'Is that right, Danny?' giggled Splinter. 'You dark horse! You never told me that you had a girlfriend.'

'Get *lost*, Splinter,' growled Danny. 'She's not my girlfriend.'

'That's not what Jonathon thinks!'

Danny scowled at his cousin. Then, to make things worse for Danny, Todd didn't hesitate to express his interest in Trinity.

He said, 'Well, I reckon she's class, boys. I wouldn't mind her being *my* girlfriend.'

At that moment, Mick came running through the rose arch.

'Danny!' he called.

'What's wrong?' asked Danny.

Mick Wilde burst out laughing, and all the boys immediately joined in even though they didn't know what was so funny. Mick's laugh had that effect – it was infectious.

Mick finally caught his breath and said,

'You better get a hold of Heffo before your uncle Larry finds him. He's after eating all of Larry's steaks for the barbeque, and poor Regina is in floods of tears. Sorry, Jonathon,' apologised Mick. 'I'm not making fun of your mammy.'

Jonathon smiled. He could see the funny side of Mick's story, but Lowry wouldn't and she was marching out of the tennis court.

Mick and the four boys – Danny, Splinter, Jonathon and Todd in fits of laughter –

disappeared back through the arch before Lowry caught up with them. While Danny hid Heffo in Larry's garage, Mick seized the opportunity to have a chat with Todd about joining the team.

When Danny caught up again with his dad, it was apparent from his long face that Mick had failed to persuade Todd to join the team.

'No luck?' asked Danny.

Mick shrugged his shoulders at Danny and shook his head.

'I tried, son. He's a tough nut to crack.'

Danny tried to stay out of Larry and Regina's way for the rest of the day. It had been his idea to bring Heffo to the barbeque and he didn't make things better for himself when he told his aunt Regina that the only reason Heffo hadn't eaten the sausages as well as the steaks was because he only liked the good, expensive, organic ones.

As Danny sat quietly in the front seat of the car on the way home, he reflected on the things that hadn't really gone to plan for him that week.

Todd still wouldn't join the team, and to make matters worse, the new boy from down under had caught Trinity's eye, and that really worried Danny.

C h a p t e r   F i v e

'The Best Stadium in the World'

Tuesday couldn't come quick enough for Danny. It was the morning of the trip to Croke Park.

As the coach pulled away from the school gates, thirty loud and slightly over-excited pupils cheered with their hands above their heads. It was only a thirty-minute drive to Croke Park, but to Danny it felt like eternity. This was a huge experience for him. He had been to Croker many times to watch games with Mick, but now he was actually going on a tour of the stadium, and that meant getting to see areas he would not normally see. He was looking forward to it so much that he could hardly sit still in his seat.

Todd was sitting behind Danny and Splinter. There wasn't a peep out of him for the whole journey until the coach turned down Russell Street, heading for Clonliffe Road and he saw the enormous, magnificent stadium.

'WOW!' he gasped.

Danny jumped up on his seat and turned to Todd.

'It's savage! Isn't it, Todd?'

'I reckon!'

As the coach turned off Clonliffe Road and into St Joseph's Avenue, all thirty boys were looking in one direction only – upwards! The colossal size of the stadium was breathtaking.

Danny felt a tingling sensation rush through his entire body.

It must be amazing for the players, thought Danny. *I'd feel like a gladiator arriving at the Coliseum if I was going to play here.*

Danny's thoughts were rudely interrupted by Splinter's left elbow.

'Wake up, Danny. We're getting off now.'

As Principal Dunstan and Mr Breen tried to organise the boys, Billy Stapleton caught everyone's attention by announcing that a train was passing by – they were right beside the railway line.

This was to Danny's great disappointment.

'Are you off your head, Billy?' he laughed.

'What? It's the train!'

'A train!' repeated Danny. 'Forget about the train will you, and turn around and look at what's in front of you.

Not only Billy, but every single boy in Danny's class turned around and looked straight ahead.

'That's the best stadium in the world lads, and it's ours and all you're interested in is a train. Get real will yiz. Over there to the right is Hill 16, and–'

Danny probably would have given the whole history of Croke Park if Principal Dunstan hadn't interrupt him.

'Very good, Mr Wilde. If all fails you could lead the tour today.'

Danny just grinned and calmly followed the others from the back of the line. He had made his point and everyone had got the message.

There were two men sitting behind the counter in the reception area. One was fairly young and the other older. As the class from Littlestown piled in through the doors, the two men looked at each other and smiled as if to say, *here we go!*

The tour was arranged for eleven, but it was only a quarter to now, so everyone was given a small booklet of the museum floor plan, and Principal Dunstan told them that they could have a little look around at the ground level while they were waiting.

At once, everyone split up into their small groups of friends. Todd stuck close to Danny and Splinter. Billy Stapleton, however, didn't bother sticking with a group. Billy was well known for enjoying his own company.

'Horses make better company than people,' Billy often said.

'Look at all those medals!' said Splinter, pointing over to a glass case on a wall in the reception.

The three pals pressed their noses against the glass, gazing at a big display of county and all-Ireland medals that a player called Jimmy Doyle had won.

'D'ya know this bloke?' asked Todd.

Splinter shook his head and turned to Danny expectantly.

'Nope!' answered Danny. 'He was a hurler for Tipperary. 'Not my game, Todd.'

The rest of the class had scattered far around the museum, but Danny wasn't in such a frenzy. He wanted to take it all in. He was well impressed with the set up. There were large projector screens showing films of football matches, as well as small television screens slotted into the walls.

He didn't mind if he didn't get to see

everything today. *Sure my da can bring me another time,* he thought.

Just before eleven, Principal Dunstan and Mr Breen started rounding up boys from all corners. The tour guide – the older guy from behind the desk – introduced himself. He seemed to be a nice man – not grumpy or sour faced, but friendly and enthusiastic. He led everyone out of the museum and into a cinema area.

'I'm going to show you all a short film, lads. It's called *A Sunday in September*, but before I turn it on, you're probably wondering what these chairs and microphones are for?' Then he smiled, 'This is also where the disciplinary board meets!'

Splinter looked at Danny.

'What?'

'You know when you make it onto the Dubs' team?' smiled Splinter.

Danny nodded.

Splinter just laughed, then nodded toward

the seats with the microphones.

'Get lost!' laughed Danny. 'I'll never end up in here.'

The film only lasted for about ten minutes. It was clips of two All-Ireland finals in 1997. Kerry versus Mayo in football, and Clare versus Tipperary in hurling.

Although there was great atmosphere and great play in both matches, Danny kept looking over toward the guide as if to say, *When are we going to see the Dubs?*

Splinter giggled a little, and nudged Danny.

'Look at Todd,' he whispered.

Todd was getting into the film in a big way. For the first time since Danny and Splinter had known him, they were now getting to see a different Todd – one who was really enjoying himself and letting himself be enthusiastic.

Todd was leaning forward in his seat and clenching his fists. He didn't care what teams were playing. He just loved the whole exciting game that was unfolding in front of him, and when the play suddenly slowed down and a loud heartbeat noise pounded from the speakers all around the cinema, Danny thought Todd was going to keel over.

After the film, the guide led them out through a door and into a huge concrete tunnel.

'This is the service tunnel,' he said. 'I need everyone to keep to the far right as we are walking. There are quite a few vans and cars in today, so please be careful.'

Principal Dunstan backed that up with a stern look at each and every pupil.

'Are we going out to the pitch?' Danny asked. He couldn't wait to get out there.

The guide nodded. 'We'll get there. We've a few things to see first.'

As Danny walked in line along the walls of the tunnel, he wondered why they were being brought this way. It was kind of boring.

What's so special about this? he thought.

His answer came quickly.

The guide stopped at a corner of the tunnel, and pointed into another tunnel.

Danny could see the pitch!

'Animal!' he announced.

'Every corner tunnel that leads into the pitch has a name,' said the guide. 'This one is the Mohammed Ali tunnel.'

'But he's a boxer!' laughed Splinter.

Principal Dunstan gave a terrifying growl at Splinter. Splinter stepped in behind Todd.

The guide told them that Mohammed Ali had fought in Croke Park in 1972, and that was the tunnel that he walked through into the arena.

Danny got the message. The tour had already started in this concrete service tunnel!

The next corner tunnel was named after U2 because they played the first concert in Croke Park.

The tour was starting to get better as the guide led them into the player's lounge, to show them the famous Waterford Crystal

Chandelier. Danny would never have thought he could be interested in a chandelier, but this one was made of thirty-two crystal footballs and seventy-two crystal sliotars – he even thought he wouldn't mind having something like it in his own house!

Todd turned to Danny and Splinter.

'You Irish really take this GAA seriously!'

Danny nodded with pride. Todd was starting to get the GAA bug. Danny just knew it.

As they were led back out of the player's lounge and into the concrete tunnel again, Danny couldn't hold back any longer.

'Are we going out to see the pitch?' he hounded the guide.

The guide laughed.

'I bet you're going to be an all-star,' he said. 'You have only one thing on your mind. Sign of a great player.'

Danny was well chuffed.

The guide led them over to a yellow door with DR-1 written on it in large black print.

'Don't you want to get into the player's dressing rooms?' he asked, looking over toward Danny.

Danny's head nearly fell off.

'Savage!'

The door was unlocked and everyone barged into the dressing rooms. It was a spectacular moment. Every county's jersey was hanging up in the dressing room. Danny's eyes fixed on one jersey and one alone. The blue jersey with Átha Cliath on it. It was an emotional moment for Danny. This was his dream. He just couldn't believe that he was standing in the very dressing room where his heroes prepared themselves for battle.

Mr Breen organised all the boys into a tight huddle around the Dubs' jersey – to fit them all in he had to get most of them to sit or lie on the floor – and took a picture for the school's wall of memories.

After the dressing room, they passed through

a warm-up area. It was amazing – a big, white room with artificial grass on the floor and netting along the ceiling. This was where the teams practised before going out to a match.

Danny's stomach was starting to churn. He knew that the moment was close.

The guide led them back out of the dressing room area and through a short green tunnel. Finally! They were pitch side!

All the boys cheered. Danny Wilde was the loudest of all. Even Todd Bailey let out a roar of appreciation at this wonderful place.

As everyone followed the guide up to the trophy presentation area – where they were shown the President's seat, number 21, Danny, Splinter and Todd remained pitch side.

'Why isn't that corner over there covered with a stand?' asked Todd.

'History,' answered Danny.

'History?' repeated Todd.

Danny told Todd the story of Hill 16 and the Dubs and the tale of how the rubble from the

1916 Rising was used to make the Hill.

'That's sacred ground, Todd,' said Danny.

'Yeah!' agreed Splinter.

'D'ya think you're ever gonna play for the Dubs, Danny?' asked Todd.

Danny turned to Todd.

'It's my dream, man. I know I'm going to play for them. And some day, up there where all the lads are standing, I'm going to lift the Sam Maguire Cup.'

Todd smiled.

'I wouldn't mind a bit of that action too.'

Splinter looked at Danny, then at Todd.

'Then you know what you have to do, don't you, Todd?' laughed Splinter.

*   *   *

To everyone's disappointment, the tour of the stadium was nearing its end. The guide led them all up into a VIP area, then up several escalators and showed them around the media centre. Danny got one last glimpse of the pitch, before they were led back down loads of sloping paths, where they ended up back in the concrete tunnel, were the tour had begun.

With the turn of key, a door was opened and they were back in the museum again.

Principal Dunstan thanked the guide, who was nipping off for a well-deserved cup of tea, then told everyone that they could have a few minutes more to have a look around the upper level of the museum before their departure.

Even though everyone was instructed to keep quiet and orderly, the mood upstairs in the museum was chaotic. All the boys were rushing around to catch a glimpse of this and that. Danny ushered Splinter over to section number twenty-nine.

'Look Splinter. The real Sam Maguire Cup.'

Splinter looked at Danny with a bewildered expression.

'What do you mean the real one?' asked Splinter.

'That's the real one,' insisted Danny. 'It was put up here in 1988, and a replica was made then.'

'Nice one!' said Splinter.

'Where's Todd?' asked Danny. 'I have to show him this.'

Danny found Todd in section twenty-five – the internationals area.

Todd was looking at an Australia versus Ireland international compromise game.

'Did you play much Aussie rules, Todd?' asked Danny.

Todd didn't turn around. He just kept staring at the screen.

'All the time, mate,' he answered.

'Do you miss it?'

Before Todd had a chance to answer, Splinter came rushing around the corner. He was hyper!

'Come on! Yiz are missing all the fun!'

Splinter dragged them up to sections thirty and thirty-one. All the other boys were there and there was great banter going on. It was an interactive games area.

'Savage!' said Danny.

There were two kinds of green areas, leading up to two yellow and orange walls, about ten metres away.

There was netting separating the two play areas.

The right side area was for hurling.

You had to hit a sliotar at the wall and your speed was then shown above the wall.

Danny had little or no interest in this except for the fact that Mr Breen was boring the pants off a few poor unfortunates as to how to hold a hurley properly.

Not for Danny Wilde!

All the good action was in the left play area – the football area.

There were two holes in the top corners of its wall, and the trick was to kick the ball into one of the holes. It required great precision and GAA skill.

There was a great show going on here as Principal Dunstan was trying to kick the ball out of his right hand, and nearly over-balancing. He missed it a few times and nearly ended up on his ear. All the boys were in stitches.

Danny bravely stepped in to give him a bit of advice.

'You can't do it like that!' he laughed.

'Go on, Danny!' shouted Billy Stapleton. 'Shown him how it's done.'

Principal Dunstan handed the ball to Danny and humbly stepped aside.

'In your own time, Mr Wilde,' he said. 'I believe you're a bit of a dab hand at this game. Don't let the school down now.'

Word of the banter that was going on in the interactive area was filtering around the building, so some of the staff hurried up the stairs to watch, followed by a couple of German girls who were waiting for the next tour. The crowd huddled behind Danny as he held the ball and gazed intently at the top right-hand corner hole in the wall.

'This is impossible,' Todd whispered to Splinter.

Splinter looked at Todd.

'You don't know our Danny. When he gets something in his head, there's very little he can't do with a football.'

Todd watched, anxiously awaiting Danny's shot. He hoped in his heart that Danny would make the score, even though it seemed totally impossible.

Danny stepped back. The crowd of onlookers stepped back.

Hearts could be heard beating, it was so silent in that room.

Danny made his move.

He released the ball down to the outside of his right runner and kicked it toward the wall.

The ball swerved away from the netting and rattled through the hole, making a bang and a clatter as it hit the metal on the inside of the wall.

Everyone cheered as the ball shot back out through a hole in the bottom of the wall and Danny Wilde picked it up and walked back toward his principal.

Danny handed the ball to Mr Dunstan, whose jaw was still hanging open.

'Here you go,' smiled Danny and he casually left the room, followed by Splinter and Todd jumping up on his back cheering.

With that wonderful shot, Danny had capped off the perfect trip to Croke Park. There was nothing left worth seeing that would better that moment.

Chapter Six

Todd's First Training Session

Danny and Splinter talked their way through the whole training session that night on the Little Croker, telling all the other players about their amazing trip to Croke Park earlier that day.

Mick would probably not have been so easy on them if Danny hadn't told him the good news that Todd Bailey was finally considering joining their team.

'He's at least thinking about joining,' said Danny. 'He got all fired up after the tour. He's going to come up on Thursday night to training.'

Mick Wilde was chuffed. Todd could be the

bandage that he needed to repair the gaping wound up front. The loss of in-form Barry Sweeney had hurt Mick's team more than he would ever have thought.

Of course he had his subs, and it was only fair to use them, but Mick couldn't, like any good manager, resist the opportunity of getting his hands on a good player when it came along.

Mick was no scout – that wasn't the way he worked. GAA wasn't like soccer. He wouldn't be going out of his way to bring in players, but if they happened to come along by whatever luck, as Todd had, then his door was open wide.

* * *

Todd turned up for training on Thursday evening as promised. He was early and seemed very enthusiastic and raring to go. Todd's early arrival gave Danny a chance to introduce him to each player as they turned up. Mick could have done this, but he liked to give Danny these things to do. It was all part of being a captain, according to Mick, the building up of captain and player relations.

It didn't take long for someone to mention that Todd looked slightly different to everyone else. It wasn't the fact that he was bigger than all the other boys (except for big Johnner Purcell), or better-looking or anything like that, it was simply that his training gear was different.

'What kind of jersey is that you're wearing?' asked Paddy Timmons. 'It's a bit skimpy. How come it has no sleeves?'

Todd smiled as if he had known it was only a matter of time before that question would arise.

'It's my club jersey from home, mate,' he replied.

'It's mad looking!' chuckled Paddy. 'I'd be freezing in that!'

'He's from Australia,' laughed Splinter. 'They don't have to worry about the cold down there!'

All the other lads laughed and Paddy went a bit red.

'I know that. I was only saying that I'd be freezing if I had to wear it here.'

'Well, you don't have to wear it,' said Splinter, 'cos it's Todd's jersey.'

Jimmy shook his head at his son, and interrupted the two boys before things got out of hand. He knew well that Splinter and Paddy got on each other's nerves at the best of times, and he didn't want them putting Todd off the team on his first training session.

Todd didn't mind at all. He thought it was a laugh.

Once they were all out on the pitch, Mick instructed Jimmy to set out a few cones.

'I'm going to break them up into a couple of groups, Jimmy,' he said.

Jimmy, like the good assistant he was, nodded.

'The first group,' continued Mick, 'I want you to get them working on picking up the ball without breaking their stride.'

'Nice one,' said Jimmy.

'You can feed the ball to them. Nice and fast now, Jimmy. Make them work hard, and sprint them back around to the back after they've fisted the ball to you.'

'And the others?' asked Jimmy.

Mick had to think for a second. Jimmy could tell that there were a good few things that Mick had on his mind for the boys to practise; the poor start to the division had Mick's thinking cap working extra hard.

'Em … I think we'll get them to work on their weaker foot. Right kickers can pass the ball to the opposite end with their left and lefties do the opposite.'

'Sound, Mick. I'll stick with the first group and keep an eye on the others.'

Jimmy was great. He knew exactly what Mick had in mind when he saw him call Danny and Todd over to him. Mick was going to see just how good the boy from down under was.

Mick started off by throwing a few balls in for Danny and Todd to contest.

Todd was bigger and stronger than Danny, but Danny was no ordinary player. Mick had selected him, not because he was his son, nor even because he was the team captain, but because Danny was probably the best player Mick had and he needed to see how Todd would compete with that.

Todd impressed him very quickly.

He won some balls, though Danny, through pure talent as he was inferior in size, won some as well. But Mick saw at once that Todd was tough, brave and up for a good hustle. Mick liked these qualities in a player.

'Have a breather, lads,' said Mick after a couple of throws, 'I'm going to kick the ball along the pitch and get yiz to compete for it.'

Danny nodded and then grinned at Todd. Todd smiled back in a kind of respectful way.

Mick kicked the ball.

All the other players stopped in their tracks;

Jimmy let them as this was something that nobody wanted to miss.

Danny was a little faster than the Aussie and got to the ball before Todd, but just as Danny had clipped the ball up into his hands, Todd, in a moment of madness, forgot that he was supposed to be playing GAA and not Aussie Rules – CRASH! Todd stormed through Danny – legs, arms, everything – he used every limb and muscle to knock Danny flying through the air. Poor Danny let the ball go – he'd been on the receiving end of many bad tackles before, but this one was different. It was like being hit by a rhino.

Jimmy ran over to Danny who was having difficulty catching his breath.

'Ya headcase!' shouted Kevin Kinsella.

'Kevin!' yelled Mick, and he made a *Shut it!* gesture at the player.

Mick left Jimmy to look after Danny and walked over to Todd who was looking ashamed, and a bit nervous. Mick didn't want a scene. He knew that Todd wasn't like Sean 'Dirty' Dempsey who he'd had to expel from the team last year. Todd was just used to playing his own sport – Aussie rules. Mick knew that Aussie rules allowed much more contact in play, so he understood that there was no bad intent on Todd's part.

'Don't worry, Todd,' said Mick as he patted him on the shoulder.

'Sorry, coach,' Todd apologised, then he turned around and put his hand out to Danny.

Danny was fine. No injuries, thankfully. Todd had just knocked the wind out of him.

Danny shook Todd's hand then looked at Mick.

'I think we've a bit of work to do with this one, Da!' he laughed.

Todd laughed too.

'Sorry Danny, mate. I'm up for it, if you give me a chance.'

Danny threw his arm around Todd.

'Don't worry Todd. We'll make a GAA

player out of you yet.'

Mick told Danny and Todd to join in with Jimmy's groups. He knew, all joking aside, that Danny was right. He had a lot of work to do with Todd if he was going to keep him on the field without getting a red card.

After training, Todd went around to Danny's house to get a form from Mick.

Danny, Splinter and Jonathon sat outside on the wall with Todd as Mick went in to get the form.

'Here we go, Todd,' said Mick coming out with the form, 'just get your mam and dad to sign it and get it back to me as soon as possible. I don't think we'll have it through for the next league game, but we'll definitely be okay for the Féile.'

Todd was a bit confused. *What's a Fay le?* he thought. *I'll ask Danny to bring me up to speed about it.*

Glancing down at the form, Todd asked Mick if just his mam's signature would be all right.

'Is your da dead?' asked Splinter. The moment he'd spoken Splinter couldn't believe those words actually crossed his lips. He was thinking them, but he hadn't meant to say them out loud.

'Shut up, Splinter,' said Danny, looking quickly at Todd to see if he was upset.

Todd smiled.

'No, mate. My parents are separated and I'm over here with just my mum.'

Mick jumped in before Splinter said something else to embarrass him.

'Ah! That's fine, Todd. Your mammy's signature will do. No worries.'

Just then Larry drove up the road to collect Jonathon.

Perfect timing! thought Mick.

Larry shouted out to Mick as Jonathon opened his door,

'Is the game still on this weekend?'

'It is indeed!' answered Mick, waving to his brother.

'I'll see you then!'

'Come to the match on Saturday, Todd,' said Mick as he turned to walk back into the house. 'It will be good for you to see us in action.'

'Okay, coach,' said Todd.

Mick peeped out through the curtain after he made himself a nice cup of tea.

Nice one Danny! he thought as he watched his son show Todd a few GAA moves on the road.

Splinter had gone in, but Danny was putting in extra effort with Todd, and that made Mick very proud.

He knew Todd needed all the help he could get if he was going to be ready in time for the Féile on 23 May.

Chapter Seven

Littlestown Crokes v Rockmount

Todd had arranged to meet up at Danny's house on Saturday before the match. By the time he arrived, Mick and Danny had already been out to the Little Croker to repaint the lines and hang the nets.

'Todd!' said Danny, opening the door to his friend, 'Come on in.'

'Ah, Todd,' greeted Mick, 'Have you got that form for me, son?'

Todd reached into his tracksuit pocket and pulled out the crinkled form and handed it to Mick.

Mick glanced over the form quickly, just to make sure that everything was in order.

'Clifford Road?' said Mick. 'Is that where you're staying?'

Todd nodded.

'We're staying with my mum's Aunt Peggy.'

Mick smiled.

'It's about a twenty-minute walk from here. Yeah! I know it.' Mick turned to Danny and smiled. 'Your mammy and I used to rent a house there for a while after we got married, Danny.'

Sometimes Mick would mention little memories like that about Danny's mam. Danny liked to hear them; he couldn't really remember his mam, so things like this made her seem more real to him.

Whenever something like this happened to Mick, he would always be in great form afterwards, and this made Danny happy too.

Mick was whistling now as he ran up the stairs.

'I'll be back in a minute, lads. Get the bags out to the door, Danny.'

'Does your mum come to the games?' Todd asked Danny as they picked up the bags.

From the look on Danny's face, Todd knew instantly that something was wrong.

'Sorry, mate. I didn't mean to be nosy,' said Todd.

'You're grand, Todd. It's fine. My mam died when I was a baby.'

Todd felt awful now. He'd half expected Danny to say that his mam and dad were separated too, and in that split second that Danny had paused before answering, Todd had hoped that they *were* separated. At least then he would have that in common with Danny.

Mick came running back down the stairs, still whistling.

'Are the bags not out yet?' he laughed. 'Step aside, lads. Let Super Coach take care of them.'

Danny and Todd laughed at Mick.

Everything's all right! thought Todd. *I haven't hurt Danny's feelings.*

That was important to Todd. Danny was

beginning to become a good mate, and Todd knew deep down that he needed a good mate.

Over at the Little Croker, Todd hovered outside the dressing room while Mick was giving his players their pre-match talk. He felt a little awkward – he was the new guy, and it didn't seem right just yet for him to be involved in dressing room preparations.

Mick was almost finished drilling his players.

'This is the last league game before the Féile kicks off in two weeks, boys. Do your best, lads and try and enjoy the game.'

'No game next week, Mick?' asked Doyler.

Mick shook his head. Then he said,

'Actually ... listen up, boys. We're going to have a short game ourselves next Saturday – normal match time. It will keep us sharp.'

Mick was thinking that Todd needed to get a match behind him before the Féile competition. This would be a great opportunity for that. Then looking around the room, he noticed for the first time that Todd was missing.

'Where's Todd?' he asked Jimmy.

Jimmy shrugged his shoulders.

'He's outside,' answered Alan Whelan, Crokes' centre half back.

Mick opened the dressing room door.

'In you come, Todd,' instructed the coach. 'Don't be hanging around out there. You're one of the team now.'

Todd shuffled his way past Mick, and squeezed himself in between Danny and Splinter who had pushed aside to make room for him.

Suddenly Mick's phone rang. Normally Mick would never take a phone call in the dressing room, during a match or even when he was training his players, but he'd left his phone on this time, because Todd wasn't the only player missing from the dressing room – Jonathon was also absent.

Larry's name flashed on Mick's phone.

'Where are yiz?' Mick asked anxiously.

Jimmy looked worried for a few seconds

until he heard Mick say,

'Right! I'll meet yiz at the pitch. Is he in his shorts and boots? Nice one. Hurry up, Larry!'

Mick hung up.

'They're almost here – got delayed,' he said.

*   *   *

As Mick and Jimmy followed the team over to the Little Croker they could see Larry and Jonathon belting up the grassy bank towards them.

Jimmy handed the number eight jersey to Jonathon.

'Here J,' he said. 'Come on. I'll do a little warm up with you.'

Mick scowled Larry.

'Don't blame me!' said Larry holding his hands up. 'We're always early, and we would have been today if those two hadn't decided to tag along.'

Two heads appeared over the horizon of the

hill – two girls' heads. Strolling along, linking each other and giggling, were Lowry and Trinity. This was the first time they had ever come to see the Crokes in action.

*   *   *

Rockmount GFC had been out on the pitch for almost ten minutes already, and they were starting to get impatient.

Mick ran over to their manager to apologise and then he did the same to the referee. Mick's team was always out on the pitch on time, and Mick holding out for Jonathon's arrival had not made him popular.

Danny Wilde stood in front of his opponent and, for the first time ever, he found himself distracted before the throw in. Instead of his usual eye-balling to put the other player off, Danny found himself staring over at Trinity.

'Danny!' whispered Jonathon.

Danny turned to his cousin.

Jonathon just nodded towards Rockmount's midfielder, as if to get Danny to concentrate.

'What are they doing here?' asked Danny.

'I'll tell you later,' said Jonathon. 'Don't mind them. The ref's going to throw in now.'

Jonathon was right, Danny needed to concentrate, so with a great effort he turned away from the sidelines and looked at the other team. The referee threw the ball in, Danny jumped and, yet again, managed to win the throw in.

He fisted the ball down to Jonathon, but Rockmount's number nine beat him to it, and kicked it along the ground to his number eleven who sweetly clipped it up and fisted it powerfully over to number ten, the right half forward.

Number ten was Rockmount's star player. Danny recognised him from the Dublin Development Squad – his name was Dennis Dolly, and having seen him in action, Danny knew he was going to be trouble for the Crokes.

Dolly turned Karl O'Toole, Crokes' left half back, with ease and went on a solo. He was fast – very fast. Not that dissimilar to Danny.

The crowd was going wild over at the Rockmount side.

'Go on Dolly – fleece them!'

And Dolly did just that, twisting and turning around Alan Whelan, then sending a perfect left-footer shot over for a point.

Rockmount were already in the lead!

You could sense the tension from the Crokes' line. Jimmy had already started on biting at his fingernails – well what was left of them from the last match – and Larry had already untied Heffo from the training bag and gone for a walk up the line so that he wouldn't have to watch.

'Come on, lads!' roared Mick. 'Get stuck in!'

Danny snapped into super mode. He had two motives that were geared up for one out come – victory.

The two motives – Trinity and Dolly.

There was no way Danny was going to be

humiliated by letting his team be slaughtered in the very first game that Trinity Dawson came to see, and neither was he going to give Dennis Dolly the opportunity to brag to the rest of the Dublin development squad that his team was better than Danny's.

Danny played a stormer in the first half. He rallied his players together and really lifted their game.

The Crokes' supporters really got behind Danny, they cheered, screamed out his name and yelled for the team. And on the sidelines, Todd watched a master in action and was humbled – and determined to learn to become a GAA player like Danny Wilde.

Danny scored two points and set Splinter and Doyler up for two more each.

Even little John Watson, who had well and truly been thrown in at the deep end at centre half forward, scored a lovely point after Danny threw a shimmy around Rockmount's centre half back, releasing Watson free to shoot.

Rockmount's weaknesses quickly unfolded. Their one and only strength was indeed Dennis Dolly. Once Mick Wilde realised this, he yelled constantly at the Crokes to keep the play away from Rockmount's gifted number ten.

That tactic worked as Rockmount only scored one more point in the first half.

As the referee blew his half-time whistle, Crokes were winning comfortably by a score of 0-7 to 0-2.

'Get the oranges out, Jimmy,' smiled Mick, who was very happy with his team's first half performance.

All the players drained every drop of juice from their well-deserved oranges and then crowded in close to listen to Mick.

'Nice one, lads,' praised Mick. 'That's great playing out there. They're a one-trick pony,' he continued, referring to Dennis Dolly.

'Keep him out of the game boys and you'll stay on top for this one,' added Larry.

Jimmy chewed on his lower lip. *There goes*

Larry again, he thought. *Stuff this! I'm going to say something as well!*

'Yeah!' said Jimmy and nothing else came out.

All the players started tittering.

Poor Splinter was mortified. *Is Da losing the plot?* he thought.

Mick just looked at Jimmy, expecting something else, but nothing came – not a word.

Although Jimmy had great intentions to say something, he hadn't enough time to work out what to say.

The referee blew his whistle for the second half.

'Right, lads,' said Mick. 'Back out there, and don't drop your guards. Keep the ball away from you know who. We don't want him getting back into the game.'

Everyone ran back onto the pitch, except Danny who was standing as if mesmerised, looking over at Todd laughing with Trinity and Lowry. Danny didn't care about Todd being friendly with Lowry, but Trinity was leaning into Todd, laughing at what he was saying, and that bothered Danny.

'Danny!' yelled Mick to snap his son out of his trance.

Danny jumped.

'The game!' said Mick with a shocked look on his face.

Danny ran out to the centre of the field.

'I'll jump for this Danny. Is that okay?' asked Jonathon, but Danny didn't answer. He was still staring over at Todd and Trinity.

The ball was thrown in and Jonathon jumped high and strong, but he was beaten to it. Rockmount's number eight caught it easily and kicked it long up field.

Jimmy ran over to Mick's side.

'What's wrong with Danny?' fretted Jimmy.

Mick looked over his shoulder and nodded towards Todd.

'I think Romeo there is getting a bit too close to Lowry's friend for Danny's liking.'

'Ah, Jaysis, Mick!' said Jimmy. 'We can't have that. We need Danny. I'll have a word.'

'Leave it, Jimmy,' said Mick. 'I'll have a chat with Danny myself. Just go over and try and get Todd to look at the game. He's supposed to be learning about GAA, after all, not trying to get young Trinity's telephone number.'

Jimmy walked slowly along the line, peering at Todd out of the corner of his eye. He didn't want to barge over and embarrass Todd. He thought he'd wait a moment or two and see if Todd would notice him and maybe give the two girls the brush-off.

As Jimmy tried to get his attention, he couldn't help overhearing Todd telling Trinity something very interesting,

'Yep! My mum and dad are separated quite a while now,' began Todd.

'What happened?' asked Trinity. 'Did they not get on with each other?'

'Nah! It wasn't really like that,' said Todd. He paused and then continued,

'I suppose you could say we were all victims of my dad's success.'

'Really?' said Trinity. 'What does he do?'

Todd paused again before saying,

'Oh, he's a top Aussie Rules coach. He travels around a lot and I guess he and Mum just grew apart.'

Trinity was impressed, and so was Jimmy.

'He used to play professionally when he was younger,' added Todd.

'Do you miss him?' asked Trinity.

'Kind of, but we keep in touch on the phone a lot, and send e-mails and stuff.'

Suddenly Jimmy heard Mick calling him. He ran back up to Mick and began to tell him everything he'd heard, but although it was interesting stuff, at the moment, Mick was more concerned about the fact that his team seemed to be losing their grip on the game.

In those few moments that Jimmy had been listening to Todd talking about his dad, Rockmount had scored a point. To make things worse, Danny's lack of concentration was damaging the rest of the team's form. With Danny off-form, Dennis Dolly was back in the game, and he was going to make the Crokes pay for his first-half exile. Dolly won every ball that his team mates played over to him, knocking over point after point and sending in long, precise passes to his full forward line.

There were only a couple of minutes left on the clock and Crokes had a narrow lead of only one point with a score of 0-8 to 0-7.

Mick hollered words of encouragement to his team to hang on, but hang on they couldn't and Rockmount stole a draw from the Crokes with an equalising point scored by none other than Dennis Dolly!

Mick asked Jimmy to gather all the players in the dressing room, while he and Danny took down the nets. Jimmy just nodded. He knew that Mick was anxious to have a little chat with the team captain.

Mick waited until everyone had left the

pitch before he brought up the tender subject of Trinity Dawson.

'What happened out there, Danny?' asked Mick.

Danny looked down. Mick had never seen his son this low after a game. Of course the Crokes had lost games before, but Mick knew that this wasn't only about losing the game. He didn't want to jump straight into the conversation about Trinity though, he'd prefer to let Danny open up by himself.

'It's nothing, Da,' said Danny as they rolled up the net.

'It didn't look like nothing to me. Something was bothering you out there, Danny. I've never seen you distracted like that before.'

'I know. I just had a bad game,' muttered Danny.

'Did somebody do or say something to put you off?' asked Mick, trying to get Danny to come clean. Mick knew what was bothering his son, but he also knew that girl business for a teenager was serious business and it had to be dealt with carefully.

Danny didn't answer straight away. Mick thought he was going to get it all out in the open.

'I'm grand,' said Danny. 'Just an off-day.'

'It wasn't anything to do with Trinity being here, was it?' asked Mick.

Danny went red.

'Trinity!' he gasped, 'No way, Da. Not a chance. I mean ... was Trinity here? I didn't even see her!' pretended Danny.

Mick could see that he'd embarrassed Danny, so he decided to leave it at that.

'Sorry, son. Just a thought,' he said

By the time Mick and Danny joined the others in the dressing rooms, the whole team was excitedly discussing Todd's dad, the famous Aussie Rules coach. Todd wasn't in the dressing room; there was no sign of him at all.

'Hey, Danny!' said Darren Ward, Crokes' right half back, as he was tying his shoe. 'Did you hear about Todd's da?'

Mick looked at Jimmy accusingly. Jimmy immediately buried his head in one of the training bags to hide from Mick.

'Where's that pump, I thought it was in here. One of the balls is soft. Now where is it?' fumbled Jimmy.

Mick smiled. He couldn't but love Jimmy, even if he did have a big mouth from time to time.

'What about Todd's da?' Danny asked Darren.

Just then, Todd walked in through the door.

'There's Todd now!' said Darren. 'Hey! Todd! Nice one about your da. That's animal, man!'

Todd looked a bit bewildered.

'What's it like having a da who was a pro Aussie player, and is now a top coach?' smiled Kevin Kinsella, Crokes' left corner full back.

Todd laughed a little, but it was a nervous laugh and he went a bit red too.

'Is that right Todd?' asked Danny.

'Eh … Aw … Yeah, Danny. Crikey! It's no big deal, boys.'

Danny walked over to Todd and patted him on the shoulder.

'Savage, Todd,' smiled Danny. 'No wonder you're a good player.'

Then Danny sat down and started to get himself changed.

Mick was pleased with Danny.

Maybe this Trinity business won't be such a problem after all! thought Mick.

Chapter Eight

An Important Meeting

Later that night, Danny came home from Splinter's house to find Mick flapping around the house in search of a pen.

Mick was on his phone.

'Danny!' he called, 'Where are all the pens?'

Danny ran upstairs and took a pen from his schoolbag and handed it to Mick.

Mick rushed off into the kitchen, and started jotting down notes on the back of an envelope.

The next twenty minutes were quite mysterious as Mick made and received several phone calls. Finally he called Danny into the kitchen and asked him for his help.

As a result, Danny went into school on Monday morning with a mission – a mission for

Mick; Mick had received an important phone call and it required the urgent attention of Principal Dunstan.

Danny arrived at school early, and went straight to the principal's office at the end of the first and second year's corridor. He knocked on the door.

There was no reply.

Danny knocked again. *Where is he?* he thought. *The Grim Reaper is always in his office.*

Thankfully, Danny didn't say those words aloud as Principal Dunstan came tiptoeing along the corridor and stood behind Danny without Danny even hearing him approach.

'You're looking for me, Mr Wilde?' he asked.

'Aaagh!' screamed Danny nearly jumping out of his skin, 'I didn't hear you.'

The principal just smiled, satisfied with the boy's surprise. It had taken him many years of practice to master the art of sneaking up on pupils. Oh, yes! Principal Dunstan had caught many a pupil up to mischief with this skill of his.

He let Danny into his office.

Although Danny was coming to the end of his first year in secondary school this was his first time in the office. Danny looked all around the room as Mr Dunstan twiddled with his computer. Being old-fashioned, he didn't actually know how to use the computer very well, but every morning he switched it on just for the sake of doing so.

After a while of button-twiddling, the principal's head reappeared from behind the computer monitor.

'Now, Danny. What's the trouble?'

'Nothing!' replied Danny.

The principal looked at him in surprise.

Danny tried again,

'I mean … my da …' he stuttered. He wished that Mick had come in to talk to the Grim Reaper himself. Danny wasn't comfortable at all in this one-to-one conversation and, to make things worse, he kept thinking of how he had showed Mr Dunstan up last week in the interactive games room in Croke Park.

'Is your father okay?'

'Savage! … I mean, he's fine …' answered Danny. 'He was wondering if he could … Well not just him, but the club – our club – Littlestown Crokes, our GAA club … He was wondering if we could sort of have a loan of your school hall on Thursday night after training … my da wants to call an important meeting with all the players' parents.'

Danny took a big breath of relief. There! He had managed to get it all out!

Principal Dunstan smiled. He appreciated the effort Danny was making for his football club.

'Certainly Danny,' he agreed, 'but he'll have to bring the hall back to the school when he's finished with it. Is that okay?'

Danny just looked at him for a few seconds.

What's he on about?

Then he realised that Principal Dunstan was actually being humorous.

Savage, thought Danny, *but weird! The Grim Reaper's not supposed to be funny.*

Principal Dunstan raised his eyebrows in anticipation of an answer from Danny.

'Great. I'll tell my da. That's super. Thanks very much. He'll be over the moon.'

*   *   *

Mick had a great turnout for his meeting in the school hall. He had asked all of his players on Tuesday night to ask their parents to attend his meeting after training on Thursday and most of them came along. Some of the other managers from the club were there too, as well as all of Mick's players. This meeting concerned everyone.

Mick sat at a table at the top of the hall with Jimmy sitting to the right of him and Maurice Clarke, the club's president sat on his left. Danny and the rest of the team all sat together at the back of the hall.

Mick began to speak once it appeared that everyone was settled in their seats.

'Thanks everyone for coming tonight. I think I know you all. For anyone I don't know, and who doesn't know me, I'm Mick Wilde, the manager of the under-14's team. This is Jimmy Murphy, my assistant and to my left is our club president, Maurice Clarke. I'm sure you all know Maurice,' smiled Mick. 'Now, I have some good news to announce. The boys have probably mentioned the Féile. They all seem pretty excited about it – that's probably the reason why most of you are here – and I'm delighted they're looking forward to it so much. The main reason I called everyone here tonight is that I'm going to need your help and support if what I have to propose is going to work out …'

Mick went on to tell everyone that Cherrydale, one of the two teams who were supposed to host the under-14's Division 1 County Féile could no longer do so due to pitch vandalism problems.

'We've been asked if we want to step in. I know Cherrydale's manager very well,' smiled Mick, 'and he'd be thrilled if we took over the hosting from them.'

Everyone looked at each other. Littlestown to host the Féile? The boys from the team could hardly sit still they were so excited. Splinter started cheering and had to be hushed by Jimmy who stood up and frowned at him.

A man put his hand up. It was Paddy Timmons' father, Charlie.

'I think that's great news, Mick,' said Charlie Timmons, 'but we don't have much time to get ready for this. The Féile's only a little over a week away.'

'Well! I think if we all pull together as we've done in the past for whatever reason, we certainly can do ourselves proud,' answered Mick.

Both Jimmy and Maurice, the club president nodded in agreement and support of Mick's answer.

Another hand went up.

It was Dolores Darcy, mother of Liam Darcy, the Crokes' goalkeeper.

'Howya, Mick!' greeted Mrs Darcy.

'Ah! Howya, Dolores, I didn't see you there behind Johnny Kinsella's big head!' laughed Mick.

Everyone joined in, especially Johnny Kinsella, Kevin Kinsella's dad. He and Mick were good pals.

Dolores Darcy took a few minutes to calm herself before she could ask Mick her question.

'Sorry, Mick,' she said. 'You had me in stitches there. I was wondering how are we going to do this when we don't have anywhere for these people? We don't have a clubhouse, Mick. Sure that's why we're all sitting here in the school hall now. Surely we're not going run the whole show from here, are we?'

Mick smiled.

'Good question, Dolores. No, we're not, that wouldn't work. To be honest, I don't really know. That's one of the reasons why I asked everyone here tonight, to see if we can work something out together.'

Another hand went up. Mick was starting to feel the pressure already.

It was Alan Whelan's father, Gerry.

'Do you have any idea, Mick, when we're getting the new clubhouse and dressing rooms. I thought we were supposed to have them this year?'

Now things were getting a little side tracked. This wasn't what Mick wanted. He needed everyone to come up with solutions as to how they were going to co-host the County Féile, and that as yet wasn't happening.

Maurice Clarke, the club manager, picked up on this and stepped in.

'Sorry Mick,' apologised Maurice. 'Could I answer that one?'

Mick was delighted.

'Hello everyone. As Mick kindly introduced me earlier. I'm Maurice Clarke, the club president. Just to answer that question from … is it

Mr Whelan? No plans have changed for the new build. The grants are all through and we've been in discussion for some time now with various builders and have finally appointed a contractor to carry out the works. We're hoping to get going on the project before the end of the year or maybe start early next year and we're all very excited about the whole thing!'

Everyone seemed happy with Maurice's answer. Splinter was so delighted with the idea of the new dressing rooms that he started punching Jonathon and Danny and had to be hushed again.

Another hand went up from the very back row of seats.

Mick couldn't make out the person's face.

The man stood up, so Mick could see him better.

It was Larry! Mick hadn't noticed Larry arriving, but he was thrilled that his brother had made the effort. Things between Mick and Larry were great now since they sorted out their differences at the end of last season.

'Larry!' smiled Mick. He was dying to know what Larry was going to ask.

First, Larry introduced himself to everyone; he was used to that, being a barrister.

'I'm Larry Wilde. Mick's brother. My son Jonathon plays on the team.'

Jonathon was scarlet. *Get to the point dad, before you bore them to death!*

Larry continued,

'It seems to me, looking at the turnout here tonight, that everyone who has some form of attachment to the club – whether their child plays for Mick's team or they're managers or whatever – you all obviously care a lot about each other.'

'Have you any questions Larry?' Jimmy blurted out.

Mick scowled Jimmy. He knew that Jimmy wasn't getting on too well with Larry, but this wasn't the right moment for that nonsense.

'Not really!' answered Larry. 'I have a

suggestion if that's alright?'

'Go ahead, Larry,' encouraged Mick.

'Well, I think that you have all the ingredients to co-host this Féile with great success.'

Everyone listened attentively.

'You have commitment, passion, pride, support. The only thing you don't have is a large room for refreshments and maybe a couple more dressing rooms for the teams.'

'That's a big problem,' laughed Charlie Timmons. 'You can't expect everyone to eat sandwiches and drink tea on the pitch. What if it rains?'

Larry paused for a second or two, and then he smiled.

'I wouldn't dream of suggesting that! I have a golfing friend who owns a marquee rental company. He owes me a favour. I'm sure he wouldn't mind lending you a large marquee for a refreshments tent, and maybe a smaller one too, if you like. You'd be under canvas in case it rains, and you could set out tables and chairs and so on. I think that would sort that problem out for you!'

Mick nearly jumped out of his chair. He turned to Maurice Clarke. Maurice nodded, with a smile as big as a Cheshire cat.

'Ah! Larry. That'll be great!' said Mick.

'I don't know about permits or whatever you might need to erect them in the park,' said Larry.

'I'll take care of that,' said Maurice.

'Will your friend throw the sandwiches and teas in, as well?' laughed Dolores Darcy.

Larry shook his head. He wasn't sure whether Dolores was actually being serious or not.

'Ah, well! That's that, girls,' said Dolores. 'Don't make any plans for going out next Friday night. It looks like we'll be making the sambos for this Féile.'

Everyone laughed.

That was that! Everyone agreed to help out now that Larry had solved the one and only obstacle that stood in their way.

Larry the hero! thought Mick. He was very proud of his brother.

*　　*　　*

As the school hall emptied out, Mick noticed Todd walking over towards him with a woman.

'Coach!' said Todd. 'This is my mum, Sarah.'

That name sent Mick's mind wandering. Danny's mother had also been called Sarah.

'Pleased to meet you, Mick,' said Sarah. She had an Irish accent, with a hint of Australian to it.

'Sarah! Yes! Nice to meet you too,' said Mick – his voice trembling slightly.

'I just wanted to thank you for having Todd on your football team.'

'Not at all,' said Mick. 'We're thrilled to have him.'

Danny walked over.

'Da, Mr Dunstan wants to know if anyone wants tea?'

'In a second, Danny. I'm just talking to Todd's mam.'

'Hi Danny,' smiled Sarah. 'Todd's been telling me all about you.'

Mick could see Principal Dunstan anxiously waving over to him.

'I'm sorry, Sarah,' apologised Mick after the interruption, 'Would you like a cup of tea?'

'Sorry Mick. We have to go. My aunt is at home on her own.'

'Well, it was very nice to meet you. I'll see you again some time.'

'That'd be nice,' smiled Sarah.

Mick went over to where Mr Dunstan was serving tea. He turned around to wave goodbye to Todd and Sarah, but they were already gone out the door.

Chapter Nine

'An AFL Coach?'

It was Saturday 16 May and there was just one week left before Littlestown Crokes were to co-host the county Féile.

There was no game on that day, but Mick had arranged for all his players to meet up for an hour's training, just to keep them sharp. After warm-ups and a few exercises with Jimmy, Mick set up a smaller pitch on the Little Croker and split the boys into two teams to play a half-hour friendly match – fifteen minutes each half. That was the length of a match in the Féile and Mick thought this would be a great opportunity to get a look at Todd's progress.

'That's superb, Todd. You're getting it now,' praised Mick as he watched the game.

Todd had come on really well. All Danny's hard work with him was paying off. It was obvious to Mick and everyone else that Todd was a talented footy player and that he was gelling into the sport of GAA very quickly.

'Call them in, Jimmy,' yelled Mick.

Jimmy was acting as referee, which gave Mick a chance to concentrate on his players. The boys ran over and crowded around, listening attentively to Mick.

'Right, boys. Well done. I don't have to remind yiz that the Féile kicks off next Saturday–'

'Do you think we can win it, coach?' asked Liam Darcy.

'Of course,' answered Mick.

'But we're not doing that well in the league.'

'Look, boys,' said Mick. 'If *you* believe you can win it, then *I* believe you can win it. Whatever teams we're playing in the first round, at least we're playing them here on our own turf. That's a great advantage. Isn't that right,

Jimmy?' asked Mick.

'That's right, Mick. And there'll be great home support boys. That'll give yiz a real boost.'

'Exactly,' agreed Mick. 'The main thing is that you enjoy the whole experience and whatever result comes out of all this, myself and Jimmy will be very proud.'

All the boys cheered. Mick was great at building up their confidence.

'Okay, boys,' he finished. 'Same time for training on Tuesday. Great work today. See yiz all then!'

Danny had arranged with Jonathon and Todd to go back to Splinter's house and play on the PlayStation for a while. As they were about to head off, Mick called Danny over.

'Danny, son,' he said, 'will you give Jimmy a hand to bring all the stuff back to the house. I'm heading off to the shopping centre from here. I want to pick up a few messages for your granny. She hasn't been able to get out since she picked up that cold.'

Danny nodded.

'Yeah, sure. If Splinter and J and I all help we'll be finished in no time!

* * *

Mick was standing by the soup section, close to the end of the aisle, when suddenly he heard an enormous clatter coming from the other side. Mick chuckled a little to himself, then felt a bit guilty for laughing at the poor person on the other side who had obviously knocked a load of tins over.

I think I'll see if they need any help! thought Mick.

As he turned the corner and looked down the peas and beans aisle, he could see a very flustered woman down on her knees trying to pick up tins of curried beans which had been in a 'special offer' display and were now rolling all over the floor.

Mick knelt down to help her.

'Your knight in shining armour!' he joked.

The very embarrassed woman lifted her head and smiled. To Mick's complete surprise it was Todd's mother, Sarah!

'I knew I remembered that voice from some-where,' she joked.

Poor Mick's cheeks looked as if they were on fire.

'Todd's mam!' stuttered Mick. 'Sarah! I didn't know it was you.'

'Does that mean you wouldn't have helped me if you did?'

'Oh no!' answered Mick. 'I mean, yes!'

Mick was getting a bit flustered now.

'I'm only pulling your leg,' Sarah smiled. 'Thanks for helping me, especially as nobody else bothered.'

Mick smiled. He looked like a teenager in love for the very first time.

*　　*　　*

Sarah had persuaded Mick to let her buy him a coffee for helping her. She felt it was the least she could do, and although Mick really should have been getting back to his mother's house with the shopping he accepted without any hesitation.

'Have you been in Australia long?' Mick asked her as they drank their coffee. 'Only you still have a bit of a Dublin accent.'

Sarah nodded. She couldn't answer straight away as her mouth was full of cream doughnut.

'Quite some time. Most of my life actually,' she eventually answered. 'I moved over there with my mum and dad when I was fifteen. So, I suppose about twenty-three years now.'

'You look very young for your age' said Mick.

Sarah blushed.

'Oh! I wasn't trying to embarrass you,' said Mick.

'It's fine,' said Sarah. 'I haven't had such a nice compliment in a long time.'

Mick really liked Sarah, and he wanted to get to know more about her.

'Are you separated long from your husband?' he asked.

'About a year,' answered Sarah. 'How did you know?'

'I overheard Todd mention it.'

'It's great that Todd has joined your football team. He really loved his footy back home. It'll be good for him,' smiled Sarah.

'He's settling in great. It must be hard for him having to leave his footy behind especially seems that his dad is a top coach in the AFL,' said Mick.

Sarah lifted her head from sipping her coffee.

'Excuse me?'

Mick just stared back at Sarah, wondering what he had said wrong.

'Todd's dad isn't an AFL coach!' laughed Sarah.

'He isn't?'

'No! He's a motor mechanic.'

'Oh!' said Mick, looking very surprised.

There was silence for a moment or two, then Sarah spoke again.

'That's really funny. What made you think that Todd's dad is an AFL coach?'

Mick wasn't sure whether he should answer that question, but after one look at Sarah's worried face he knew he had to.

'Overheard that too,' he said.

'Todd was telling somebody that?' asked Sarah.

Mick nodded his head.

Sarah looked very worried now.

'Is everything okay, Sarah?'

'I'm not sure,' said Sarah.

Mick looked confused.

Sarah opened up to him about how they had come to be in Ireland.

'Todd's dad and I have been separated for about a year. Todd took it very badly at the beginning. It looked like he was just about getting used to us living apart, but then Scott met another woman.'

'Oh!' said Mick, raising his eyebrows.

Sarah continued.

'Don't get me wrong. I was fine. I had moved on. Scott and I had grown apart over the last few years of our marriage. We just sort of fell out of love, I suppose.'

Sarah appeared to drift in thought.

Mick waited patiently. He knew that this must have been difficult for her, but at the same time he felt good that she was telling him this.

'Poor Todd,' said Sarah, putting her hands to her face.

Mick reached out his hand and touched her arm for comfort.

Sarah smiled.

'I'm okay. Sorry Mick. You don't need to be hearing all of this.'

'No! It's fine,' said Mick. 'Get it all out. You'll feel better. Trust me. When my wife died, I kept a lot of my pain inside. You're better off talking about things. A problem shared is a problem halved,' smiled Mick.

Sarah smiled too.

'His dad used to go to all of his footy games, but when Valerie came on the scene, Scott just seemed to lose interest in Todd. That had a bad effect on Todd. He even insisted on changing his surname from Bradshaw to Bailey, when I decided to go back to my maiden name.'

'Ah!' said Mick.

'Scott is a good father – he always was. He's coming over next month to see how Todd is settling in.'

'Really?' said Mick with a hint of disappointment.

'Todd started getting involved with some bad kids in Australia, he was getting into trouble a lot. He got expelled from school, Mick.' Sarah looked to Mick with real guilt as if it was all her fault.

'You're not to blame,' comforted Mick.

'Really!' said Sarah. 'I should have done more. I didn't realise at the time that he had strayed so much. He used to be such a good, happy boy. That's why I brought him here. I received word from Ireland that my aunt Peggy was ill. She was my dad's sister. My parents are both dead,' added Sarah.

'Sorry to hear that,' said Mick.

'Anyway! Here we are, back in Ireland.'

'Are you here to stay?' asked Mick.

'Not sure. I was hoping that a break from home or a new start for Todd would do him good, but if he's spinning these lies to his new friends, he's obviously still very angry with Scott. I'm worried, Mick.'

'Don't be,' said Mick. 'I'll keep a good eye on him. He's on the team now and he has this big competition coming up.'

'The Féile!' said Sarah.

'That's the one,' said Mick. 'It'll do Todd the world of good. He'll be grand.'

Sarah smiled. Mick had put her mind at ease.

*   *   *

Later that evening, while Mick was getting the dinner, Danny said something to him that set off alarm bells.

'Todd's a bit of a weirdo, Da.'

'How's that Danny?' asked Mick, while reaching for the salt.

'He just stormed off in a huff earlier from Splinter's house.'

'Why?'

'I don't know,' shrugged Danny.

'Something must have happened!'

'Not really! Splinter had got a hold of a book from the library. It was a book on all the AFL coaches and players, present and past. He kept asking Todd to point out his da.'

Mick nearly let his fork drop.

'Then what?'

'That's when Todd freaked. He got really angry. He just knocked the book out of Splinter's hand and stormed off. It was mad!'

Mick had a big decision to make.

Should I tell Danny the truth? he thought. *Maybe I'd better!*

So Mick went ahead and told Danny everything that Sarah had told him.

'Keep it to yourself, Danny,' he warned. 'I only told you so you know what's going on with Todd. You have to give him time, son.'

'I will,' said Danny. 'I can't believe it though. It was all lies about his da being an AFL coach!'

'I'm warning you, Danny' said Mick. 'You can't tell anyone. It won't help Todd.'

Chapter Ten

An Unexpected Visitor

Danny did just as Mick asked and kept Todd's secret to himself; when he saw Todd in school on Monday morning, he didn't let on that he knew a thing.

Todd apologised to Danny and Splinter for his outburst in Splinter's house on Saturday.

'It's sound, Todd,' said Splinter. 'I can understand. You probably used to get a lot of kids hassling you about your da, back in Australia – him being famous and all that. I think it's savage that your da is famous.'

Todd just smiled and nodded.

For the first time, Danny could see that Todd wasn't telling the truth; his smile was false.

Once Todd caught up with Jonathon at

training the following day and apologised to him too, Danny could see the relief on Todd's face.

This is really bothering him! thought Danny. *I think all this lying is hard for him. He seems to really need us as his friends, otherwise he wouldn't have made such an effort to say sorry!*

Tusesday night training went ahead as planned for Mick and his players.

Mick had his players well and truly fired up now for the Féile.

He couldn't have been happier – until Thursday came along.

It was the last training session before the big competition and Todd hadn't turned up.

Mick had a word with Danny after training.

'This isn't good, Danny.'

'I know,' agreed Danny. 'He didn't turn up at school today either.'

'What?' said Mick. 'Why didn't you say so son.'

Danny shrugged his shoulders.

'We're going to have to go around and see if he's okay. He might have hurt himself or maybe he's sick.'

'He didn't look sick when he was in school yesterday.'

'Did you notice anything wrong with him, Danny? Was he upset or anything?'

Danny shook his head.

'No, he was in animal form. Probably the best I've seen him in since I've known him.'

Mick and Danny hopped into the car and drove to number twenty-seven Clifford Road.

'Seventeen, nineteen, twenty-one … there it is!' pointed Danny. 'Todd's mam's outside!'

Sarah was sitting on the wall of the front garden, reading a book.

Mick rolled down the window and smiled out.

'Hi, Mick,' greeted Sarah. 'Hi, Danny.'

'Eh! We were just … I mean, Danny here was worried about Todd,' said Mick, 'and I just brought him around to see if he's okay. Danny was saying that he wasn't at school and when he didn't turn up at training–'

'He's fine,' interrupted Sarah. 'His father arrived last night and it was a bit of a surprise for Todd – he was so excited to see him he couldn't go to school or training.'

Mick felt a bit bewildered. *I thought Todd was angry with his father!* he said to himself.

Sarah winked at him.

'Oh!' said Mick. He got the feeling that Sarah was only pretending that Todd was delighted to see his father because she didn't know that Danny knew the whole story.

'Would you like to go in and see Todd, Danny?' asked Sarah.

'Not if he's with his father,' said Mick. 'We don't want to disturb them.'

'It's fine,' said Sarah. 'Scott's been out cold for the past couple of hours – jet lag.'

'Animal!' said Danny, and he got out of the car.

'Just a few minutes, son!' said Mick.

As Danny went into the house, Sarah immediately began telling Mick how she'd telephoned Scott at the weekend to tell him about Todd.

'Scott was very upset,' said Sarah.

'I can imagine.'

'But it was a bit of a shock to us all when he turned up at the house late last night.'

*　　*　　*

There was no sign of Todd as Danny walked through the sitting room and out into the kitchen.

He noticed the back door was open, and as he was just about to walk out into the garden, he heard voices – loud voices.

Todd and his dad were having an argument!

I thought his da was asleep! thought Danny as he hesitated just inside the back door.

'Can't ya just be happy, mate, that I'm here?' said Todd's dad.

'Nah! Why should I be?' said Todd.

'Aw, come on, son. Can't we put all this behind us and start again. I'm really looking forward to seeing ya play in this tournament at the weekend.'

'You're not coming,' said Todd.

'Come on, Todd. I'm after taking annual leave to be here. Come on, mate. It'd be like old times. I'm dying to see ya in action again. I tell ya what. We could go down to the local park tomorrow arvo and kick a bit of footy, if ya like?'

Todd kicked a stone and it ricocheted off a wall and nearly hit his father.

'It's not *called* footy here. It's GAA. Now rack off, ya loser.'

'Don't talk to me like that, mate. I'm still your father.'

'It'll never be like old times. You screwed that up for all of us when ya decided to get a new girlfriend!'

Todd was getting really angry now.

Danny didn't know what to do. *Todd really hates his dad!* he thought, *I shouldn't be here listening.*

Suddenly, Todd turned to come back into the house.

'Todd!' called his dad, but Todd didn't turn around.

Danny jumped back and acted like he was only just coming into the kitchen.

'Danny!' said Todd.

'Hiya Todd,' smiled Danny. 'Your mam sent me in. I just came around to see if you're okay.'

'I'm fine, mate – fine.'

Scott walked in to the kitchen.

'G'day,' he said.

'Eh, howya!' said Danny.

This was a very awkward moment indeed.

'Aren't ya going to introduce me to your mate, son?' smiled Scott.

Todd just stood still as if he was frozen to the spot.

Danny put out his hand to Scott.

'I'm Danny, Todd's friend. We're on the same football team.'

'Pleased to meet ya, Danny mate. I'm Scott, Todd's father. I guess ya gathered that already!' said Scott, shaking hands.

'Yeah! Todd's told me loads about you.'

As soon as the words were out of his mouth, Danny realised he shouldn't have said them. Todd's face went as white as a ghost. So white that Danny thought he was going to throw up on the kitchen floor.

'Really?' said Scott. 'All good I hope.'

Danny didn't know what to say or do next and it was a blessing that Sarah came into the house just then.

'I think your dad's waiting for you, Danny,' she said.

'Sound!' said Danny. He was delighted to have an excuse to leave.

'We're putting up the bunting and all tomorrow night for the Féile, if you want to help us?' Danny looked to Todd.

'Yeah, mate. Sure! I'll see ya in school tomorrow.'

'Nice one,' smiled Danny.

'See ya, Danny!' said Scott, waving. 'Nice to meet ya, mate. I might see ya at the footy on Saturday.'

Todd scowled his dad.

'You too Mr …. I mean, Scott,' said Danny, making a quick exit.

Chapter Eleven

Littlestown Pulls Together

By Friday night – the eve of the County Féile on the Little Croker – there was a real buzz around the neighborhood. All the neighbours had really pulled together for their local club.

Everyone hung out their blue bunting; it was the same bunting that everyone in Littlestown always hung out for the Dubs' big games, but as the colours matched the Littlestown Crokes as well, it was perfect for this occasion.

Mick and Jimmy had hardly been off their mobile phones, ringing around organising everything. They felt like they'd spoken to every man, woman and child in the area!

There were cups and plates and cutlery being polished for the big event the next day. Mothers and fathers and brothers and sisters were making sandwiches and baking cakes and buns, neighbours were lending knives and forks and helping to set up tables for the refreshments.

Everyone attached to the team was pulling together.

Todd hadn't taken up Danny's invitation to come down to his road and join in the preparations, but he at least rang him on his mobile and confirmed that he would be at the Little Croker, at 9.30 am – forty-five minutes before the first game, which kicked off at 10.15.

On the Saturday morning, it was a spectacular scene on the Little Croker. Hundreds of people had turned out to support their local club, in fact, it looked like everyone in Littlestown had turned up to cheer them on. The sun was shining, the bunting was fluttering in the breeze, and Larry's friend from the golf club had turned up trumps! There were two spacious marquees erected beside the old dressing rooms, a large one for the refreshments and a smaller one to be used as an extra dressing room. Crokes only had two dressing rooms for teams and a third smaller one for the referees. Larry's friend had asked his employees to erect a division down the middle of the small marquee, to make two more dressing rooms.

Everything was accounted for and all was going smoothly – except that Larry was starting to get on Dolores Darcy's nerves in the refreshments marquee!

Mick had his team in their old home dressing room and he was going through the match schedule list with Jimmy, which had just been handed to him.

It read:

10.15
Littlestown Crokes V Darnville
Terrystown V Cherrydale

(half-hour break)
11.15
Littlestown Crokes V Cherrydale
Darnville V Terrystown
(half-hour break)
12.15
Littlestown Crokes V Terrystown
Darnville V Cherrydale

Mick nodded to Jimmy.

'Okay, boys! Listen up,' said Jimmy as the players were tying up their boots. 'I have the schedule here lads. We're up against Darnville in the first match.'

Mick could hear little whispers of concern coming from his players. Darnville had already beaten them in the league.

'Settle down, lads,' said Jimmy.

'We're playing them on the Little Croker this time,' added Mick. 'The second game, we'll be on the far pitch against Cherrydale.'

At this, Mick's players started grinning at

each other. They had beaten Cherrydale in the league in their first game.

'Who are we playing in the last game, Mick?' asked Splinter.

'Terrystown – back on the Little Croker for that one.'

There was no reaction at all from Mick's team. They hadn't played Terrystown in the league yet, but they knew that they were a decent side as they were in third place in the league.

The referee popped his head in the door and nodded to Mick.

'On our way, ref,' smiled Mick. Then he turned to his team. 'Okay, boys! I want yiz all to forget about our poor start to the league this year. Yes, I know that we have to beat the very same teams that we've struggled against, but we're starting this Féile with a clean sheet. We can do this, lads. One step at a time. If we can get through this stage – these three games – then we can concentrate on the semi-final over at Chapel Hall's grounds later today, and who knows where we might go from there.'

'To the final in Parnell Park tomorrow!' cheered Jimmy, firing the players up.

All the lads cheered.

'When you go out onto that pitch, lads. Where are yiz playing?' roared Mick.

'THE LITTLE CROKER!'

'And how do we play every game?'

'LIKE THE ALL-IRELAND FINAL!'

Chapter Twelve

Féile on the Little Croker

Darnville joined the Crokes at the exit of dressing rooms area, and both teams jogged onto the Little Croker together.

Terrystown and Cherrydale had already left their marquee and were warming up on the far pitch.

Mick pulled Danny aside while the other players warmed up with Jimmy.

'How's Todd's form?' asked Mick.

'Savage, Da,' answered Danny.

'Are you sure? He seemed a bit quiet in the dressing room.'

'He's fine. I think he's just a bit nervous, you know, because this is his first time playing in a real GAA match.'

'I suppose you're right, Danny. We're certainly throwing him in at the deep end.'

'Don't worry. I'll get him into the game early. I'd say he'll be okay once he gets a few passes to him. He's an animal player, Da.'

Danny was true to his word. From the very second the ball was thrown in, he made sure that Todd was brought into the game. Mick had left Doyler in Barry's regular position, centre full forward, and put Todd into centre half forward. Todd rewarded Mick and his teammates for their belief in him, scoring two super points from long range.

Todd was much stronger than his marker, and his experience of playing in the slightly more physical sport of footy was standing to him, but at the same time Mick had worked tirelessly with Todd to pare down his rough edges, and it was showing.

The first half of the first game flew in. It was only fifteen minutes – much shorter than a regular match.

Even though Todd was playing brilliantly and Danny and Jonathon were putting in their usual great performances in midfield, Darnville led at half time, with a score of 0-2 to 0-3.

By the time the teams had come off the pitch and the Crokes were crowding around Mick and Jimmy, Jimmy had just heard the half time score of the other game.

'Terrystown are slaughtering Cherrydale!' he said.

'What score?' asked Todd.

'A goal and three points to one point,' laughed Jimmy, 'they must be playing a stormer up there.'

This won't help! thought Mick, *they're getting distracted.*

'All right boys! Settle down. Don't mind the other game yet. That score is irrelevant to us at this stage. Let's just concentrate on winning this game first,' Mick looked to Jimmy.

'Yeah! You're right Mick,' agreed Jimmy. 'Come on lads. Listen in now.'

Mick didn't have much time to talk. The Féile games were a quick turn around.

'I'm telling yiz, we can beat these fellas. Danny, I want you to push up a little more son – Jonathon will cover for you.'

Danny looked mystified.

'We need to go for it, son. We have to show Darnville that we're not afraid of them. We need to attack them from the start with everything we've got and get scores. It's only fifteen minutes.'

Danny nodded, even though he was worried about opening up a gap in midfield for Darnville. *I hope Jonathon can manage!* he thought, but he had to trust his dad. After all, Mick knew what he was talking about. He was a brilliant coach.

Danny let Jonathon jump for the second half throw in. He thought that if Jonathon could win the ball and feed it down to him, then maybe he could get started straight away on that quick attack that Mick wanted to see.

'Ready number eight?' the referee looked to Jonathon. 'Number nine?' he then looked to the Darnville midfielder, who just nodded, then quickly turned his eyes back to Jonathon.

'Strong jump, Jonathon!' encouraged Danny.

The ball was thrown in.

Jonathon jumped so high for that ball that he felt like he was stretching every tendon in his legs to the point of snapping. The second Jonathon passed the ball to Danny, Danny was away as fast as lightning. His super-fast pace left not only his opposite midfield marker for dust, but Jonathon's too.

Darnville's centre half back had left Todd free to try and stop Danny in his tracks, but Danny was too sharp and too clever for him.

Danny pretended to fist the ball over Darnville's number six, then shimmyed around him with ease. Then he heard a distinctive Aussie voice.

'Over here, Danny!' called Todd as he advanced toward the goal, his back half-turned to Danny and his left hand out beckoning a pass.

Doyler – Crokes' centre full forward – pulled his marker to one side, opening up a gap for Todd to run into.

Danny kicked the ball to Todd.

'Go for goal, Todd!' yelled Danny.

As a footy player, Todd's instinct would always be to go for goal. Maximum points in a score were always the best option if there was a chance to be taken, and that's what he had in mind.

Good on ya mate! thought Todd as he caught Danny's pass.

Todd thundered toward the Darnville goal. He looked unstoppable, and only Darnville's keeper was in his way.

As Darnville's goalkeeper threw his body toward Todd to block his incoming shot, Todd tricked him by pretending to shoot. The

Crokes' new number eleven then cheekily fisted the ball high over the keeper's head.

Everyone on the Crokes' line watched anxiously as the ball fell down towards the open goal, but it bounced off the cross bar away from the goal.

'No!' screamed Jimmy.

'Go, Jason!' roared Mick.

Jason Delaney – Crokes' right full forward was doing exactly what Mick always said he should do – he was following up the attack regardless.

Jason sprinted towards the ball, which was just coming to a stop.

His marker was tight on his heels and to make things worse, Splinter's marker had left him free and he was now nearer to the ball.

Just as Splinter's marker – Darnville's right full corner back – was about to kick the ball up-pitch and to safety, Jason stretched his left leg out to try and block the clearance.

The ball ricocheted off his boot and shot out

to the far side of the goal area into Splinter's path. Splinter clipped the ball up into his hands, took one look at the empty goal and then – BANG! Splinter sent the ball crashing into the back of the Darnville goal!

There was tremendous cheering from the Crokes' line.

This was the type of courage and determination that Mick wanted to see from his team. They were playing the second half in style!

As the Crokes' players congratulated Splinter, Mick nodded to Jimmy.

'We're on the move, Jimmy,' he said.

Splinter's goal certainly got Crokes on the move; Darnville were caught cold, and didn't really recover.

Todd added another great point to the two he'd gained in the first half and, to add to Darnville's misery, both Doyler and Jason Delaney scored a point each.

With Danny back into midfield alongside Jonathon as a result of Splinter's goal, Darnville struggled to repeat the good win they achieved over Crokes in the league.

They only scored two more points.

Crokes won their opening game in the Féile by a score of 1-5 to 0-5.

Up on the other pitch, Terrystown had easily beaten Cherrydale by a score of 2-7 to 0-3.

Mick's players had played a tough first game, and they appreciated their half hour rest before they headed over to the far pitch for the second match.

Mick started the second match against weaker side Cherrydale with the same team.

By half time Crokes were leading with a commanding score of 2-3 to 0-1, so Mick decided to make a few changes so as to give his subs a chance to play.

This slightly weakened Mick's side, but once more, Danny took total control of the game, distributing magnificent passes to his forward line and creating scores from almost every attack.

The crowd went wild! All along the Crokes line they were jumping up and down and screaming!

Crokes won the game on the far pitch easily, with a score of 3-5 to 0-2.

They had beaten Cherrydale by an even bigger margin than Terrystown had done, and that gave Mick and his players a real confidence boost.

Terrystown had one of their best players injured in their game against Darnville and this affected them badly. They just barely managed to scrape a win with a narrow marginal score of 1-4 to 1-2.

As everyone relaxed during the half hour break before the final games it was obvious to all that the two teams going forward to the semi-finals later in the day in Chapel Hall's grounds, were Littlestown Crokes and Terrystown.

But there was a lot still to play for ...

Mick was trying to get this message through

to his team in the dressing room a few minutes before the third match throw in.

'Now, if there's anyone who thinks they're too knackered or injured to start the game, please let us know now,' said Mick.

Nobody spoke out. Mick knew well even if someone was unfit to play, they probably wouldn't say anything because everyone wanted to be involved in every game.

'Are you sure, Big Johnner? That was a bad knock you took in the last game.'

'I'm sound, coach. I ran it off.'

'That's a nasty bruise,' noticed Barry Sweeney, who had popped in, broken collarbone and all, to lend some support.

'Shut up, you,' whispered Big Johnner.

'I know we're through to the semis, lads,' said Mick. There was a big roar from his players.

'Oh! Calm down, boys,' said Jimmy. 'Let Mick finish.'

Mick nodded a thank you to Jimmy.

'It's all still to play for boys,' continued Mick.

'The difference between finishing top and finishing second in the group is colossal. Top place plays the second place from the group over in Chapel Hall and their top team plays second in our group.'

'We don't care who we play, Mick!' yelled Paddy Timmons. 'We'll take anyone on!'

Everyone cheered again.

Mick had to smile and so did Jimmy. Mick didn't encourage over confidence, but he felt at this point there was no need to calm his players down too much. He relished the fact that his team were all fired up and so he joined in with their cheers, saying,

'That's the spirit, Paddy!'

This is the fire I need from them if they're to beat Terrystown! he thought.

Chapter Thirteen

Littlestown Crokes v Terrystown

People were filtering in and out of the large marquee, enjoying the scrumptious refreshments that Dolores Darcy and her posse had prepared. There was a real carnival atmosphere, and everyone's enjoyment was increased by how well the Crokes were playing.

As the Crokes' ran out onto the Little Croker for the last time in their co-hosting of this year's Féile, they heard Todd's name being called from the sidelines – it was his parents.

'Who's that with your mam?' asked Splinter. Then before Todd could answer, he said, 'Is it your da, Todd?'

That caught all the Crokes' players' attention. They all started staring over and talking at once; to Todd's horror, some of them wanted to go over and meet this so-called famous AFL coach who had come all the way from Australia.

Mick jumped to Todd's rescue, instructing his players onto the pitch.

He had bought Todd some time for now, but he knew that it was only a matter of time before Todd would be right back in this awkward predicament once again.

From the very start of the match, Danny and Mick noticed that Scott's presence at the game was affecting Todd's concentration, just the way that Trinity's had affected Danny in the Rockmount game.

I hope he snaps out of this! thought Danny watching in horror as Todd seemed to forget all he'd learned about GAA and inflicted a nasty tackle on the Terrystown centre half back as the two of them were going in for a loose ball.

Todd was lucky this time. He got off with a

warning from the referee.

The Terrystown captain and number ten, stepped up to kick a superb point.

Crokes struggled after that to get the ball out of their own half and Terrystown knocked over another four points in the space of seven minutes.

Danny and Jonathon reacted very well to the pressure with a point each to keep their opposition in reach before the referee blew his whistle for half time.

Mick didn't have any bad words for his players in his half time talk. He knew they were exhausted. Three games in one day, with the thoughts of a monumental semi final to follow was indeed a big ask, and Mick appreciated the effort they were making. He was well and truly proud of them.

As the referee threw the ball in for the second half, Mick paced up and down the line wondering if he should take Todd off and stick one of his subs on. It was a tough decision to contemplate, but the last thing Mick wanted was for Todd to be sent off.

If that happened, the Crokes would be down to fourteen men, and then it would be almost impossible to beat Terrystown, who had opened up a first half lead of three points with a score of 0-5 to 0-2.

After a pretty uneventful first ten minutes, with no further scores, something very unexpected happened.

As Brian O'Reilly, Crokes' left half forward kicked a long and sweet low pass to Todd, Todd's father roared out from the side line.

'C'mon Todd, son! Show 'em what you're made of!'

It was as if a switch suddenly flicked in Todd's brain. He caught that ball and turned his marker so quick that the Terrystown centre half back fell clumsily to the ground.

With that, Todd went on a powerful solo, shouldering off the opposition's full back as he tried to stop him.

Once again, there was just the Terrystown goalkeeper between him and the goal!

The spectators cheered along the Crokes' sideline, roaring their support for the boy from Oz.

'Go on, Todd! *Go ON!*' they screamed.

Danny watched and prayed that Todd would score. He knew that there were just a couple of minutes left and a goal would level the game.

Even a point! thought Danny. *Anything to give us a chance.*

As the Terrystown goalkeeper came out to put Todd off his shot, Todd Bailey released a devastating shot from his right boot.

The ball thundered past the Terrystown keeper, almost burning the tips of his fingers until it finally smashed the top left corner of the net.

'What a beauty!' Scott roared from the sideline.

The whole crowd were jumping up and down the line.

Even some of the Cherrydale supporters were looking down from the far pitch to see who had scored. By the time, everyone had settled again, the referee gave it about two minutes and then he blew his full time whistle.

It was a draw with a score of 1-2 for Crokes and 0-5 for Terrystown.

As all the players shook hands, Mick and Jimmy were in serious discussion with the Terrystown managers as to who should go top.

Mick saved the good news for the dressing room,

'Both teams finished with two wins and a draw,' he announced. His players waited in anticipation. 'But because we've scored a total of twenty-seven points over the three games and they only scored twenty-five, we're first in the group!'

The dressing room was filled with cheering and whistling – the Littlestown Crokes were first in the group!

Chapter Fourteen

Crosstown Trip

Once they'd all calmed down a bit from the news that they were first in the group, Mick sent all his players over to the large marquee for well-deserved refreshments.

It was one o'clock and they had a few hours rest before their semi-final which started at four o'clock, across town in Chapel Hall.

All the players tucked into Dolores Darcy's delicious sambos – but they didn't think much of her home-made paté!

Despite the morning's festival of football combat, everyone seemed to get on really well together. All the other teams' players praised Crokes and Terrystown on their advancement to the semis. This was the kind of thing that made Mick and all the other coaches so proud to be involved in GAA – here they were, all celebrating together and supporting each other.

Todd's dad was ambushed by some of Mick's team for autographs, but luckily for Todd, Scott reluctantly went along with his son's lies. Sarah was unhappy about him doing so, but Scott had already decided that if this situation arose, then he wouldn't embarrass his son in front of his teammates.

'I'll be gone back to Australia in a couple of weeks,' he had said, earlier that morning. 'There'll be no harm done.'

Some of the crowd stayed behind to help with the clean up, but most of Crokes' loyal supporters hopped into their cars to travel across town for the semi-final.

'We should have organised a coach,' said Jimmy, as they were arranging lifts for players.

'Don't worry, Jimmy,' smiled Mick. He was

in top form. 'We'll be fine. Anyway, I have Dessie Dunne and his coach on call for tomorrow's final.'

'Nice one, Mick,' smiled Jimmy. 'Fingers crossed we make it to the final!'

'Fingers and toes, Jimmy,' laughed Mick. 'Fingers and toes.'

Chapel Hall's grounds were roughly a thirty-minute drive across the city, if the traffic was light.

Mick was second last to leave the Little Croker behind. Larry had delayed him by asking him to hold on for Regina who was on her way over with Lowry, Trinity and Trinity's brother, Sebastian. Larry had to wait around the Little Croker for the men to come and pack up the marquees, so Regina wanted to follow Mick's car over to the next match.

Eventually, Mick couldn't wait any longer.

'We have to go, Larry,' he said. 'They'll just have to follow you over after you're finished your business with your marquee pal – if he ever gets here.'

Larry agreed, and Mick, Danny and Todd headed off in Mick's car. Todd's parents drove behind them in the car Scott had hired for a couple of weeks.

Everyone else was miles ahead of Mick, but he was relaxed. The traffic was light and there was plenty of time. Mick was singing along to his car radio and the lads were laughing at him and messing around when suddenly what looked like smoke came pouring out of his bonnet, and his car slowed down.

'You're *kidding* me,' cried Mick as he pulled over to the side of the road.

The car just wouldn't start again.

'I told you this banger would clap out some day,' said Danny.

Todd thought it was very funny, but Danny was worried.

'What are we going to do?' he asked.

The smoke had cleared and Mick's head was under the bonnet.

'You're wasting your time, Da. You know nothing about cars.'

'I know!' said Mick, slamming the bonnet closed.

Just then, Scott pulled in behind them.

Mick looked at Danny with an *Are you thinking what I'm thinking?* look.

Scott jumped out of his car.

'Problem, Mick?

'It just stalled on me,' said Mick, scratching his head.

'Give us a gander,' said Scott and he lifted the bonnet and disappeared behind it for a few minutes.

Mick kept looking at his watch.

'Don't worry, son. We've loads of time,' he reassured Danny who was giving him the evil eye.

'Eh … my dad is handy with cars,' stuttered Todd to Danny.

Danny just nodded. He knew very well that Scott was a mechanic, and that if Mick didn't know that as well, then he would be on his phone right now, getting Jimmy back to collect them.

'Start her up there, Mick,' instructed Scott.

Mick's car started first time and there was no more smoke.

'I've bought ya a bit more time with her,' laughed Scott. 'But you'll have to get her sorted out good and proper mate.'

'Nice one, Scott,' said Mick. 'Come on, boys, back in the car. Jimmy will be having kittens!'

Todd's dad smiled at him, but Todd didn't smile back as he got into Mick's car.

'Give him time,' whispered Sarah.

Scott was gutted, and didn't speak a word for the rest of the drive to Chapel Hall.

*   *   *

Half of Jimmy's fingernails were chewed clean off by the time they arrived at Chapel Hall.

'What kept yiz?' asked Jimmy.

'We broke down,' said Danny.

'Relax Jimmy, my oul' flower. We're here now, thanks to Todd's dad.'

'Todd's dad?' said Jimmy. 'What did Todd's dad do?'

But Jimmy was left standing without an answer as Mick, Danny and Todd hurried after the Chapel Hall manager to their dressing room, where the rest of the team were already getting changed.

Mick got quite a reaction from his team after he announced that they were to play Barnfield – their old rivals – in their semi final.

'Chapel Hall topped their group,' said Mick. 'They'll play Terrystown.'

Mick could see Danny and Jonathon nodding to each other after they learned that they were playing Barnfield.

Mick knew that his two midfielders would be up against their adversaries, Sean 'Dirty' Dempsey, who used to play for the Crokes and Deco Savage, who was just as dirty a player as Sean.

As the Crokes team ran out onto the pitch to face Barnfield, every single one of Mick's players got an electric rush through their bodies as their cavalry of supporters cheered them on.

Out of the corner Danny noticed Trinity – Larry and Regina had just arrived in their cars. Danny didn't even try to see if Todd and Trinity looked at each other.

That's not important now! he thought, *for the next half an hour this match is the most important thing in my life!*

In midfield, Dempsey and Savage were doing their best to put Danny and Jonathon off as the referee was checking something with the Barnfield manager.

Danny wasn't really paying attention to them. He was too busy looking at Mick eyeballing his old enemy Tommy Dempsey – Sean's troublesome dad.

This is going to be war! thought Danny.

'I see ya have Goldilocks playing up front for

yiz,' laughed Savage.

'Shut your mouth,' said Jonathon. 'You wouldn't say that to his face.'

'Yeah, I would,' muttered Savage. 'I'm not afraid of him.'

'You should be!' smiled Danny as the referee approached them with his whistle in one hand and the match ball in the other. 'Because he's going to make you two look like a pair of Girl Guides.'

Danny stepped forward for the throw-in against Savage.

'Don't try any of your elbow tricks like the last time, if you know what's good for you,' warned Danny.

'That's enough number nine,' said the referee, then he threw the ball above their heads.

Danny and Deco clashed off each other and fell to the ground as they both tried to win the ball. The ball fell to Dempsey, but Jonathon was all fired up after Dempsey and Savage's pre-match banter. Just as Dempsey was about to go on a solo, Jonathon punched the ball out of his opponent's hands and grabbed it. Then he turned Dempsey, not once, but twice, just to humiliate him and teach him a lesson.

Larry was dancing on the sideline.

I can't believe that I didn't want him to play for Mick's team, last year, and now look at him! thought Larry with pride all over his face as he watched Jonathon skip around two more players and then fist a perfect pass into Todd's hands.

Todd then punished Dempsey and Savage even further for their smart comments to his teammates by sending Crokes into an early lead with a long and accurate point.

This enraged the two Barnfield players, but their anger only caused them to make mistakes and Danny's team finished the first half in the lead with a score of 0-4 to 0-0.

Mick wasn't surprised to hear at half time that Chapel Hall was leading Terrystown by 1-2 to 0-1. They were indeed the strongest team in the league this year and it looked like they would be the ones to beat in the County Féile final, if his team could just hang in there for the next fifteen minutes or so.

Mick was giving his players his last few words of encouragement before the referee blew his whistle.

'Fifteen minutes lads!' said Mick. 'It's not the first time I've said that to yiz today, but I promise it's going to be the last. If yiz keep the heads together for this second half and keep up the hard work, you're in the final! I want yiz to keep focused out there.'

Larry had wriggled his way through the crowd and snuck in behind the team.

'This could be your finest moment, boys,' said Larry.

Not this again! thought Jimmy.

'Any words of wisdom, Larry?' asked Mick.

Jimmy's head nearly fell off. *Mick's never done that before! Why didn't he ask me that?*

'Like I said, boys,' said Larry. 'This could be

your finest moment. Getting yourselves into the final tomorrow in Parnell Park is the big achievement. Anything that goes our way after that is a bonus. It's the journey you'll look back on with pride.'

Then Mick turned to Jimmy, but the referee blew his whistle.

'Wait up, lads,' said Mick. 'Jimmy hasn't spoken yet.'

Jimmy was thrilled to bits. This meant a lot to him, but now that all the attention was on him, he couldn't really think of anything to say.

'Eh!' said Jimmy, 'I'll go with what Larry said.' Larry smiled. 'Oh and …' Jimmy continued, '… if yiz don't beat Barnfield, yiz needn't turn up for training on Tuesday!'

Sean Dempsey had stepped forward for the second half throw in against Jonathon, and had easily beaten him to the ball, knocking it down to Savage.

For the first time in a long time, Danny was outplayed by Savage, as the Barnfield midfielder managed to skip around Danny, sending a long pass across field to his left half forward.

The Barnfield number twelve then passed the ball into his centre half forward who then fisted it over his head, and over the head of Crokes' Alan Whelan, straight into the hands of Barnfield's centre full forward, who was fouled by Crokes' full back, Big Johnner Purcell.

Free kick to Barnfield.

'This looks dodgy, Mick,' fretted Jimmy.

Mick was too busy watching Big Johnner holding his leg.

'Johnner's injury is playing up,' said Mick.

Mick tried to call out to his full back, but Big Johnner pretended not to hear. He didn't want to be taken off.

'I'll wring his neck!' cried Jimmy.

On the referee's whistle, Deco Savage took the free kick. He didn't go for an easy point. That would have been the percentage shot to play.

No! That just wasn't Deco nor Barnfield's style!

Deco kicked a low, fast and furious shot toward the goal mouth, and as the injured Big Johnner tried to jump to block it, Barnfield's number fourteen out jumped him and fisted it past him for a wonderful goal.

The Barnfield sideline erupted.

'We'll have to get Big Johnner off!' said Mick.

Jimmy caught the referee's attention and after examining Big Johnner's leg, they decided that he couldn't play out the last few minutes of the match.

Mick brought on Derek Moran, and told Danny to drop back in deep, in front of Johnner's replacement to help them see out the game. Danny did just that, and although Barnfield and its two nasty midfielders tried everything in their power to level the game, Crokes miraculously held on to progress to the Féile final with a full time score of 0-4 to 1-0.

Chapel Hall had indeed beaten Terrystown. Their progression was with more ease, beating

Terrystown with a score of 1-6 to 0-4.

The celebrations went on for a couple of hours as Chapel Hall entertained their visitors with refreshments in their fine clubhouse. When the Crokes' team returned to Littlestown, rows of supporters were waiting for the heroes who had earned them a special GAA day out in Parnell Park the following day.

Chapter Fifteen

The Fight

The morning sun was shining down on Littlestown on 24 May, Féile final day.

The atmosphere around Littlestown that morning was electric. The Crokes had stepped in at the eleventh hour to co-host a successful County Féile and had also deservedly booked themselves a place in the final in Parnell Park at 3pm.

Everyone waved and gave a thumbs up to Danny and Splinter as they walked down to the local shops all kitted out in their brand new tracksuits that the whole team were given for the big event.

Just as they were going into Nailer's News Agents, they met Todd coming out with a

Sunday morning paper.

'G'day mates,' smiled Todd. He was also in his new tracksuit.

'What's the story, Todd?' said Splinter.

'Alright, Todd?' nodded Danny.

'Are ya all set for the final this arvo, boys?' asked Todd.

'Raring to go, Todd!' smiled Splinter, rubbing his hands together. 'What about you? I hope you got a good sleep last night.'

'Who's been talking to you, mate?' smiled Todd.

'No one. Why?' asked Splinter.

Todd put his arms around Danny and Splinter.

'Actually, boys. I had a bit of a late one last night,' then Todd laughed. 'Don't tell Mick, Danny. I don't wanna be dropped for the big game.'

'Where were you last night?' asked Splinter.

Danny pushed Splinter.

'Don't be a plank! He's only winding us up.'

'Is that right!' said Todd. 'Then ya better check with Trinity 'cos I was at the flicks with her.'

Splinter took one look to see Danny's reaction. But there was none.

'You're having us on!' said Splinter. 'Trinity wouldn't go out with you. Anyway, didn't Jonathon say that she's into Danny?'

Todd burst out laughing.

'Danny?'

Danny's face flamed red with total mortification and fury.

He wanted to kill Splinter for saying that and showing him up in front of Todd, and he wanted to kill Todd for laughing at the idea of Trinity being interested in him.

Splinter could see that something ugly was going to come to a head, right here and right now, so he decided to get offside.

'I'll be out in a minute. I'm dying for a drink,' he said as he disappeared into the shop.

'Sorry Danny, mate,' grinned Todd. 'I was

only joking.'

'About going to the pictures with Trinity?' asked Danny.

'Nah, mate. We went to the pictures, although we didn't see much of the film, if y'know what I'm talking about.'

'You're sad,' grunted Danny, and just as he was about to follow Splinter into the shop, Todd grabbed his arm.

'You're jealous, mate!' smiled Todd. It was a mean kind of smile.

'Get your hands off me,' said Danny and he pulled his arm from Todd's clutches.

Todd burst out laughing.

'You don't actually think she'd be interested in you when she has me to chase, do ya?'

Danny took a deep breath in through his nostrils. That's what Mick had taught him to do whenever a situation got out of hand on the pitch.

'Why wouldn't she?' said Danny. 'At least I'm not a liar, like you.'

'I'm not a liar. What are ya talking about?' Todd wasn't smiling anymore.

'You know *exactly* what I'm talking about Todd.'

Now it was Todd's turn to go red.

Splinter was standing by the counter near the open door, listening to the heated argument.

'You're a liar, Todd,' Danny reiterated.

'Shut your gob,' snarled Todd.

'Shut it for me,' said Danny. 'Yeah! Maybe you're dying for a scrap. Is that how you got kicked out of your school back in Australia?'

Todd pushed Danny.

'How d'ya know that?' Todd was raging.

'I know a lot of things, Todd.'

Splinter decided that it was time to stop watching and start doing. If he didn't get in between these two quickly, the team would probably be down two players for the final.

'I *said* shut your gob, mate.'

'You're not my mate,' said Danny. 'Mates don't tell their team mates that their da is a so-called famous AFL coach when really he's just a mechanic.'

'What?' screamed Splinter, looking at Todd. 'Your da's a mechanic?

Todd looked at Danny, and then at Splinter. He was well and truly humiliated.

'Aw! Rack off the both of ya. Ya can stuff your flamin' final. I'm out of here.'

Todd turned on his heel and ran off.

Splinter turned to Danny.

'Is his da really a mechanic and not an AFL coach?'

'Leave it, Splinter,' said Danny, but he nodded, just because he knew Splinter would keep asking if he didn't.

Danny was already regretting having revealed Todd's secret in anger; he'd just have to trust Splinter not to tell anyone.

Chapter Sixteen

Missing

It was lunchtime, and Dessie Dunne had just pulled up to the side of the Little Croker, where Mick and Jimmy had arranged for all the players to meet.

There was a trail of cars already lining the road on both sides, ready to follow Mick's army.

Mick did his roster check as all the boys hopped on the coach.

'Don't bring your bag on, Darren, son,' said Mick. 'Throw it underneath with the others, there's a good lad.'

'Is Todd on the coach?' asked Jimmy.

'Em! I don't think so. He didn't get past me, Jimmy. Hold on! I'll check again.'

Mick walked the whole length of the coach; there was no sign of Todd.

'He's not on, Jimmy' said Mick, jumping back off. 'Is he out here?'

There were only a few more boys to get on, and Todd wasn't one of them.

Jimmy walked all around the coach, then looked up the road, and down the road, on both sides.

'There's no sign of him.'

Mick looked at his watch.

'He should have been here by now. Keep an eye out for Scott's car, will you, Jimmy. They're just late.'

Jimmy waited and watched and waited some more and watched some more, but after fifteen minutes there was still no sign of Todd.

Danny and Splinter were sitting up the front in the second row.

'You better tell your da about this morning,' whispered Splinter.

Mick turned sharply. Splinter's notion of

whispering wasn't exactly discreet.

'What was that?' asked Mick.

Danny scowled Splinter, then turned to face the music.

'We had a fight.'

Mick hopped on the coach.

'Did you hurt him?'

Danny frowned.

'No! An argument, I meant. Not a real fight!'

Mick laughed, nervously, then after a few seconds of thought, he gave Danny a look he hadn't seen since the time he'd accidentally smashed Mrs Tyrell's glass house with his ball.

'You didn't, Danny?' fretted Mick, sweat pumping from his forehead. 'You didn't say anything about you-know-what?'

Danny didn't answer, but that was as good as a 'yes' for Mick.

'Ah, Danny ...'

At Mick's obvious disappointment, Danny slid down in his seat and hung his head.

Mick called Jimmy onto the coach.

'Come on, Jimmy,' said Mick. 'We're going.'

'What about Todd?'

'We'll have to pick him up at his house' said Mick. 'Fire her up Dessie – Clifford Road.'

As Dessie drove up Clifford Road, Mick could see Sarah looking out through the downstairs window.

'Over here, Dessie,' said Mick, pointing towards Todd's house.

Mick hopped off the coach and ran into the garden.

Sarah had seen the coach and was already at the open door. She didn't give Mick a chance to speak.

'We can't find him, Mick. I sent him to the shops for a newspaper this morning and he didn't come back.'

Mick had a big decision to make and he didn't have a lot of time to make it.

Should he tell Sarah about Danny and Todd's argument? Mick knew that if he did, Sarah would probably feel let down, and Mick didn't want that.

'He had a falling out with Danny this morning,' said Mick. 'Danny said that he just ran off. He's probably just sitting it out somewhere. Has he done this before?'

'No, Mick' answered Sarah, looking very worried. 'I thought Todd and Danny were getting on well?'

Mick just shrugged his shoulders. He was just about to tell Sarah the whole story about the two boys' argument when Scott came driving down the road.

'There's Scott!' said Sarah. 'Todd's not with him. He hasn't found him, Mick.'

Mick was torn – he had to get to the final with his team, but Todd was one of his players, and he was missing. After a moment's thought, he offered Sarah and Scott his help to find Todd – Jimmy could take the rest of the team to the match, and Larry would be there to help him. But Scott and Sarah insisted that he should get the boys to the stadium. There was no point in ruining their day, and after all, Todd was probably just sulking somewhere.

They exchanged mobile numbers. Sarah told Mick that she would ring him if she found Todd.

'Just hop in a taxi with him, and the club will pay for it,' said Mick. He got a jersey from his gear bag and gave it to Sarah. 'Here, Sarah. If you do find him in time for the game, get him kitted out on the way over.'

Mick felt terrible as the coach pulled away from number twenty seven Clifford Road.

I should have told her the whole story! he thought.

As the coach drove down Collins Avenue, and approached the big church on the corner, Jimmy let out an unmerciful roar from the front.

'Almost there, boys!'

Dessie Dunne swung his fifty-seater onto Clan Carthy road, then took the first left before a row of houses started.

They were at Parnell Park.

'Is that it?' asked Splinter with a hint of

disappointment, pointing to a pitch behind tall railings, right next to a building with the name, Craobh Chiaráin on it.

Danny elbowed Splinter.

'No! You muppet. That's their training pitch. Look!'

Danny pointed out his window, to the right.

'Nice one!' smiled Splinter.

Parnell Park was indeed a fine stadium, and there were crowds of people flooding in and out of the grounds.

There had been finals on all morning. Crokes' final against Chapel Hall was to be the last of the day, kicking off at 3 pm.

Mick and Jimmy guided their players down toward the dressing rooms in the far right corner of the stadium.

'Just imagine, Danny,' smiled Splinter. 'This is where the Dubs play. I feel real important. Look, everyone is staring at us!'

Danny didn't smile back. He was still feeling guilty about Todd disappearing.

I should have kept my mouth shut! he thought, as he walked along the red matting and into a corridor of the building that was lined on both sides with dressing rooms.

'In here, Crokes,' instructed one of the officials.

Mick closed the door behind him.

'What about Todd, Mick?' asked little John Watson.

'I don't know, son,' said Mick.

Jimmy came over to have a quiet word in Mick's ear as all the players ripped open their bags.

'What are we going to do about Todd?' whispered Jimmy.

Mick was looking over at Danny whose head was hanging low.

'I don't know, Jimmy' said Mick. 'It's not looking good. And poor Danny is upset, too, and we need him playing his best ...'

That wasn't the answer that Jimmy was looking for. Mick Wilde always had a solution, but it looked like he was a little lost this time.

'I have a suggestion!' said Jimmy.

Even though Mick was a bit surprised to hear this, he was all ears to whatever Jimmy had to offer.

'This has obviously affected the whole team, especially Danny,' said Jimmy.

Mick nodded.

'It's all about confidence and feel-good factor. Isn't that right Mick?'

Mick nodded again.

'Okay!' continued Jimmy. 'Why don't we tell the boys that Todd is on his way over, but he might not get here for the start of the game.'

'Go on …' said Mick.

'Well, that'll lift the boys' morale a bit, especially Danny's. We'll put Todd down for playing and pray that he does turn up so we can put him on.'

'What if he doesn't turn up?' asked Mick, looking a bit confused with Jimmy's plan.

'If he doesn't, then he doesn't,' whispered

Jimmy, 'but at least it will lift the other boys for the moment, especially Danny. We don't want them going out on the pitch like this. Do we Mick?'

Mick agreed. It was a decent plan. It was better if Mick's players started the game with as much confidence as possible. If all failed and Todd didn't turn up, well then they would just have to get on with the rest of the game without him.

'Nice one, Jimmy,' said Mick. 'Let's get them ready!'

Chapter Seventeen

A Riverside Meeting

Billy Stapleton was riding his horse down by the riverside, when he spotted some-one familiar sitting on the edge of the boat dock.

Billy pulled up beside Todd and tied his horse to a pole.

'Have a rest and a bit of grass, Vinny,' he said, then he sat down beside Todd, who was trying to skip stones across the river.

'What's the story, Todd?' greeted Billy.

Todd didn't reply. He didn't even look at Billy.

'Are you not meant to be at the final today?'

Todd grunted.

'Were you kicked off the team or something?'

Todd laughed.

'Nah, mate. I left the stupid team. They're all a pack of losers.'

Billy and Todd sat quietly for a couple of minutes just throwing stones into the river.

Todd broke the silence with a chuckle.

'Did I hear you call your horse, Vinny?'

'Shut up!' muttered Billy.

'That's a stupid name for a horse, mate.'

Todd was laughing now.

'No it's not,' argued Billy. 'Vinny's a sound name.'

'Yeah, if you're a loser!' teased Todd.

Billy pushed Todd's arm so hard that Todd nearly fell into the water.

'My *brother's* not a loser,' said Billy.

Todd was confused now.

'Your horse is your brother?'

'Are you thick or something?' said Billy.

'What mate? You just said that your horse was your brother.'

'No! I didn't. I have a brother called

Vinny, *as well!*' said Billy.

'Aw!' said Todd. Then he laughed again. 'What does your brother think of that?'

Billy went quiet for a moment, then he lifted his head.

'He doesn't know. I haven't seen him in two years.'

Todd could see sorrow all over Billy's face. Billy's eyes were watery.

'Why, mate?' asked Todd. The boy from Down Under wasn't laughing or joking or teasing Billy now.

'Never mind,' said Billy.

'Look I'm sorry for having a go. Seriously!'

Billy dropped his head again.

'He left home two years ago to go to England.'

'Why, mate?'

'Work, I suppose,' said Billy.

'Hasn't he been in touch?'

Billy shook his head.

'Aw, he's probably having such a great time over there mate. That's why. How old is?'

'He's nineteen now.'

'Don't worry mate. I'm sure when he stops partying, he'll get in touch.'

'He'll never come back.' said Billy. 'Not while *he's* still in the house.'

Todd left Billy alone for a few minutes. He sensed that there was something serious behind all of this.

'Who's "he" mate?' Todd asked, after a moment of silence.

'My da,' answered Billy, his voice breaking a little.

'Aw! My dad's a jerk as well,' said Todd. 'Looks like we're both in the same boat, mate.'

Billy lifted his head and turned to Todd.

'What's wrong with your da?'

'He and my mum split up last year and now my dad has a new girlfriend. He used to come to all of my footy games, but he stopped. I think he lost interest in me. Total loser, mate.'

Billy stared at Todd and then laughed.

'What?' asked Todd. 'It's not funny, mate.'

'Yeah it is,' laughed Billy.

'No, it's not, mate,' said Todd, but he was smiling now as he pushed Billy's arm.

'You haven't a clue, do you Todd?'

'What d'ya mean?'

'Your da is a saint compared to mine.'

'Why? What's so bad about yours?'

Billy went on to tell Todd that his father drank a lot, and his parents were always arguing.

'Everyone in the house is afraid of my da,' said Billy. 'He's always shouting. That's why I spend so much time with my horse. It gets me out of the house.'

'Is that why Vinny left?' asked Todd.

'Well he was always threatening to leave, but he finally went after a big argument. My da and my mam were shouting, as usual, and when Vinny came home and asked what was going on, my mam told him that our da had sold Vinny's watch that my grandad left him. He didn't care that Vinnie loved that watch, and that he'd always taken care of it because it used to be our grandad's, he just wanted the money. That was the last straw for Vinny. He left home two days later.'

Todd felt awful.

And I thought my dad was bad! Billy's right! thought Todd. *My dad is a saint compared to his. I've got to put things right!*

Todd jumped to his feet.

'Billy, boy!' said Todd. 'How d'ya feel about giving me a lift on your horse, mate?'

Now Billy jumped to his feet.

'Vinnie can carry two easy! Where to?'

'I need to get home, mate.'

'Animal!' cheered Billy. 'Come on Todd. Hop on.'

Todd climbed onto Vinny's back behind Billy.

'Giddy up, Vinny!' shouted Billy.

'Yee haw!' cheered Todd, as they thundered along the riverside in the direction of Littlestown.

Chapter Eighteen

The Féile Final

A short time later, as Todd and his parents raced across town in a taxi, the Under-Fourteen's Division 1 final had just started.

Mick had taken Jimmy's advice and told all the players that Todd was on his way. This had really helped Danny's morale, and he was determined not to let his team down as he battled for every loose ball.

There was a tremendous crowd in the stadium – it was packed full. Most were supporters from both teams, and some were people who had stayed on from earlier games, and the rest of the numbers were made up from GAA enthusiasts who just came down to see the division 1 final –

the big one!

Todd's absence had definitely weakened the side. Little John Watson was playing his heart out in Todd's place, but he was no match in either strength or skill for Chapel Hall's centre half back.

Chapel Hall was leading with a score of 0-3 to 0-1 when suddenly Mick's phone rang.

Mick had a golden rule, never to answer his phone during GAA business. Normally he'd have its volume turned down, and though he'd left it on this one time, he was so wrapped up in the match that he didn't hear it at first.

Jimmy nudged Mick.

'Your phone!'

'Not now Jimmy – the match!'

'It might be about Todd.'

Mick had completely forgotten! As he answered his phone, Jimmy was all ears!

'That's great!' cheered Mick. 'Yeah! It's almost half time. Get him in as quick as you can. I'll send Jimmy out to yiz.'

Mick hung up.

'Nice one, Mick,' Jimmy was rubbing his hands in delight. 'Oh no! They're after scoring another point.'

'Todd's outside, Jimmy,' interrupted Mick.

Jimmy turned on his heel and hurried to the exit – the Crokes really needed Todd now.

Jimmy came back up the line with Todd just as the referee blew the half time whistle.

Chapel Hall was leading, 0-4 to 0-1.

Mick called his team over. They were thrilled to see Todd.

Danny walked straight over to Todd.

'Alright, Todd!'

Todd put his hand out and Danny shook it.

'Sorry mate!' said Todd, 'I shouldn't have picked a fight with ya. I was jealous, because you and Mick spend so much time together, and he watches your games ...'

'I'm sorry too, Todd,' said Danny.

'Enough of that you two,' smiled Jimmy. 'Listen up!'

Mick looked straight at Little John Watson.

'Good game, John,' said Mick. 'Do you mind if I put Todd on for the second half?'

Little John shook his head.

'I don't mind, your man has my back in bits from climbing all over me.' Then he turned to Todd. 'Sort him out for me, Todd!'

'Will do, mate,' smiled Todd.

Unusually, Mick Wilde didn't have too many words of wisdom for his players. Like Larry had said on the Little Croker the day before – it was all about getting to the final. That was the big achievement.

Crokes started the second half of the final match in the County Féile just three points behind Chapel Hall.

They needed a goal if they were to claw them back.

Danny did his best to get the ball up to Todd, but Chapel Hall's defence had really gelled together and they kept the Crokes in their own half for most of the second half of the game.

Only for Crokes' two centre backs playing their hearts out and keeping Chapel Hall from scoring, it would have been the end of the road for Mick's team.

With only a few minutes left on the clock, Crokes had a free kick just inside Chapel Hall's half. Danny stepped up to take it.

Mick turned to the crowd to get them going.

Todd looked over into the stand behind Mick and Jimmy. He caught a glimpse of his parents.

They were waving at him.

Todd turned his attention back to the game.

Danny kicked the ball out wide to his right full forward, Jason Delaney.

Jason lost the ball to his marker, but then bravely won it back for Crokes when he dived at the Chapel Hall's number four and blocked his clearance with his hands.

The ball flew across into the path of Jonathon who had followed Danny's free kick. Jonathon clipped it up into his hands and kicked a perfect pass to Todd who was running towards him.

Todd decided it was time to turn on a bit of magic and show his team mates what he could really do. As his marker closed in on him, Todd turned and sprinted toward goal. The Chapel Hall number six couldn't get near him. Todd fisted the ball to Doyler, who then skillfully fisted it over his marker's head and back into Todd's path.

Todd collected the ball and took one good look at the goal. He took three more paces, dropped the ball, onto his left foot and swerved it around Chapel Hall's keeper.

GOAL!

The whole of the Crokes' section of the stadium erupted into cheers and roars of approval.

Todd went on a celebratory run back toward his captain and he and Danny and Jonathon danced in triumph.

Mick couldn't stay easy on the line. He kept looking at his watch and asking Jimmy if he knew how much time was left.

Jimmy was shaking like a leaf. If Mick Wilde was nervous then Jimmy Murphy was hysterically nervous.

Mick noticed the referee looking at his watch too.

'It's nearly up, Jimmy,' said Mick.

'Come on the Crokes!' shouted Jimmy. 'One more point and we have it!'

Those words were like a curse to Crokes as Paul Kiely, Crokes' right half forward, lost the ball to Chapel Hall's left half back. The Chapel Hall number seven sent a long pass up the line to his left half forward who turned Croke's Darren Ward and kicked a low pass into his centre full forward.

'I don't like the looks of this, Jimmy,' cried Mick.

Now Jimmy was shouting to the referee to blow his whistle.

Chapel Hall's number fourteen stared straight at the Crokes goal and kicked the ball over for a point.

'Nooooo!' screamed the Crokes' fans, as the Chapel Hall supporters went wild.

The referee looked at his watch one last time, and to Mick and Jimmy and their team and all the Crokes' supporters' disappointment, he blew the whistle. Chapel Hall were County Féile Champions.

Danny bravely held back the tears as he watched the Chapel Hall captain lift the cup.

Todd threw his arm around Danny.

'Sorry if I let you down, Danny. I should have been here for the first half.'

Scott and Sarah were walking toward them.

'It's sound, Todd,' smiled Danny. 'You're a deadly player. We probably wouldn't have got to the final without you.'

'Thanks, Danny,' smiled Todd.

'You should make up with your da,' said Danny.

'I will,' said Todd, and then he walked over to meet his parents and gave them both a hug.

Danny could see that the warmth they used

to have as a family had returned.

Danny looked over to Mick who was running around patting all of his players on the shoulders and giving hugs to the ones that were really upset.

Todd's right, thought Danny, *he is a great father, and a great coach.*

Just as Danny was jogging over to them, Todd turned and called out to him.

'Hey! Danny, mate? Trinity's crazy about ya mate. All she did was talk about you all night!'

Danny smiled and gave Todd a big thumbs up.

Then the Littlestown Crokes' captain joined the rest of his team-mates in their last few moments on this magnificent pitch, knowing in his mind that this was a big day that the team from the Little Croker would never forget.